Kelly could see him kicking his bike to life and starting to follow them before the ambulance reached the end of the street.

She cleared her throat as she received acknowledgment from her radio handset that she'd been patched through to Kensington's emergency department.

"We're coming to you with a thirty-seven-year-old woman—Vicky Tomkins," she told them. "Pregnant, almost thirty weeks gestation, sudden onset of acute abdominal pain and bleeding approximately ninety minutes ago. Suspected placental abruption. We'll be with you in about six minutes…"

Another glance through the rear window showed Kelly that her ambulance SUV was right behind the ambulance. Just beyond the SUV was a large bike with a tall man in a dark leather jacket and a black helmet.

Ari Lawson—the astonishingly different midwife who had unexpectedly dropped into her life less than an hour ago—was riding shotgun.

For some inexplicable reason that she wasn't going to allow any brain space to analyze, knowing he was close by was making Kelly feel safer. Protected, even.

And it was a good feeling.

Dear Reader,

There are many things about writing—and reading—romance novels that I love. Perhaps the most important is the affirmation that love can be powerful enough to change people's lives, to heal past hurts and to offer hope for the future.

There are times we can all benefit from being reminded of the power of love. Not just romantic love but also the love within families, whether those families are biological or chosen (and I, for one, definitely include close friends as part of my chosen family).

Ari, the hero in this story, knows about how strong the bonds within a foster family can be. And Kelly, like too many of us, has experienced an abusive relationship and the aftermath of discovering how hard it is to trust again.

The magic of storytelling let me bring these two people together. I hope you end up feeling as misty as I did to see how love worked that amazing magic of its own on Ari and Kelly—and maybe one or two other people along the way...

Happy reading!

Alison xxx

THE PARAMEDIC'S
UNEXPECTED HERO

ALISON ROBERTS

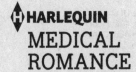

HARLEQUIN

MEDICAL
ROMANCE

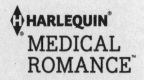

ISBN-13: 978-1-335-14943-5

The Paramedic's Unexpected Hero

Copyright © 2020 by Alison Roberts

All rights reserved. No part of this book may be used or reproduced in any manner whatsoever without written permission except in the case of brief quotations embodied in critical articles and reviews.

This is a work of fiction. Names, characters, places and incidents are either the product of the author's imagination or are used fictitiously. Any resemblance to actual persons, living or dead, businesses, companies, events or locales is entirely coincidental.

This edition published by arrangement with Harlequin Books S.A.

For questions and comments about the quality of this book, please contact us at CustomerService@Harlequin.com.

Harlequin Enterprises ULC
22 Adelaide St. West, 40th Floor
Toronto, Ontario M5H 4E3, Canada
www.Harlequin.com

Printed in U.S.A.

Alison Roberts is a New Zealander, currently lucky enough to be living in the South of France. She is also lucky enough to write for the Harlequin Medical Romance line. A primary school teacher in a former life, she is now a qualified paramedic. She loves to travel and dance, drink champagne, and spend time with her daughter and her friends.

Books by Alison Roberts

Harlequin Medical Romance

Medics, Sisters, Brides

Awakening the Shy Nurse
Saved by Their Miracle Baby

Rescue Docs

Resisting Her Rescue Doc
Pregnant with Her Best Friend's Baby
Dr. Right for the Single Mom

Hope Children's Hospital

Their Newborn Baby Gift

Twins on Her Doorstep
Melting the Trauma Doc's Heart
Single Dad in Her Stocking

Visit the Author Profile page
at Harlequin.com for more titles.

Praise for
Alison Roberts

"I read this in one sitting. This was such a heart-felt story. I loved the characters. The author really did a fantastic job…. I highly recommend this story to anyone. It was a real treat to read."

—*Goodreads* on
Pregnant with Her Best Friend's Baby

CHAPTER ONE

OH, MAN...

It was clearly going to be one of "those" days. Ari Lawson could hear the shouting as soon as he pulled his helmet off, having shut down the engine of his powerful motorbike and secured it on its stand. Checking the house numbers in this outer suburban London street confirmed that one of the people engaged in this heated argument was standing in the doorway of the address he'd been dispatched to but it definitely wasn't the person he'd been asked to check up on. This was a belligerent man in his mid-thirties—about Ari's age—who was waving his fist at the middle-aged woman from the next-door terraced house.

'Mind your own bloody business,' he was yelling.

'It *is* my bloody business,' the woman

yelled back, 'if you're punching holes in walls that I'm on the other side of. I've called the police.'

'As if they'll listen to you, you daft old bat. They never have before.'

Ari had lifted his kit from one of the panniers on the back of his bike. He walked towards the house.

'Who the hell are you?' the man demanded. He looked Ari up and down, his expression disgusted. 'Get lost, whoever you are. You're not wanted here.'

'I'm here to see a Vicky Tomkins. This is where she lives, yes?'

'There you go.' The next-door neighbour folded her arms across an ample chest. 'Vicky's called for help. 'Bout time, if you ask me.'

'Nobody asked you,' the man spat. 'And she didn't call anyone.'

'Yes, I did.'

Everybody turned instantly towards the woman now framed by the doorway behind the angry man. An obviously pregnant woman who was pale enough for alarm bells to start ringing for Ari.

'I called my midwife,' she said. 'She said she couldn't come but she'd find someone who could.' But the younger woman was sounding hesitant now. 'Another midwife…?'

'That's me,' Ari confirmed. 'Your midwife—Yvonne—is busy at the hospital in the middle of a delivery at the moment so she asked if I could come and see you. I'm a midwife, too.'

The moment's silence didn't surprise him. Ari was quite used to people finding a male midwife an unusual concept. Add in the fact that he was well over six feet tall, wore a leather jacket to ride his motorbike and kept his shoulder-length hair up and out of the way in a man bun for work hours and the reaction from others could often be a lot more than bewilderment. It wasn't the first time he'd heard something like the raucous burst of laughter from the man in front of him.

'You have *got* to be kidding me,' he said. 'A midwife? Well, you're not getting anywhere near *my* wife, mate.'

For the umpteenth time, Ari had to wonder why it was such an odd concept that the only appropriate male role in pregnancy or childbirth was that of an obstetrician. At least he was quite familiar with dealing with this kind of prejudice.

'I think that decision is up to Vicky,' he

said calmly. 'She's the one who called for help.' He caught her gaze and held it, doing his best to convey reassurance that she could trust him. 'You're experiencing some abdominal pain, yes?'

She nodded. 'And I'm bleeding,' she told him. She had a protective hand on her belly and her voice dropped to a shaky whisper. 'Please… I'm scared…'

The man wasn't about to move but Ari was a head taller and he wasn't about to let this client down. He knew she was less than thirty weeks pregnant and, if she was in pain and bleeding, she could be in real trouble. He could hear a siren not far away, which reminded him that he could well need to call for back-up sooner rather than later.

'There you go.' The neighbour sounded satisfied. 'That'll be the cops on their way and they'll sort you out. I hope they lock you up this time.'

Sirens were commonplace in any huge city and this area of London had more problems than many so Ari thought it unlikely that they would be responding to a minor disturbance like this, but Vicky's husband was incensed, stepping sideways and raising his hands as well as his voice so that he could grab the fence railing between them and shake it. Ari used the opportunity to step closer to the person who had called for help.

'Are you safe here?' he asked quietly. 'Or do I need to get you somewhere else to check what's happening?'

Vicky shook her head wearily. 'He'll settle down,' she said. 'He just gets wound up sometimes, you know?' There was curiosity in her glance this time. 'Are you really a midwife?'

'I really am. But if you're uncomfortable with that, it's okay. I can refer you to hospital for an obstetric check.'

'I don't want to go in there. I'd have to wait for hours and I'm supposed to be working tonight. *Ow...*' Vicky clutched at her belly with her whole arm as she bent forward. 'Oh, that really hurts...'

'Come and lie down somewhere.' The sound of the siren was fading rapidly as Ari put a supporting arm around her shoulders. 'Couch or bed—whatever's easier. We need to find out what's going on.'

A very short time later, he ended his phone call, hoping that he would be hearing another siren from an emergency vehicle in the very near future—from the ambulance he had just summoned.

Paramedic Kelly Reynolds shut down the lights and siren on the rapid response vehicle she was driving as she approached the suburban address she'd been dispatched to. Parking directly behind a large motorbike, she jumped out of the driver's seat to go to the back hatch of the SUV to collect the gear she might need, slipping her arms through the straps of the backpack that contained an extensive first-aid kit. One hand was then free to carry the life pack with its monitoring and defibrillation capabilities and Kelly took a deep breath as she took her first step across the road.

As a rapid response paramedic it was her job to either arrive first to assess and stabilise what could be a serious case, or back up an ambulance crew that needed expert assistance. Sending an officer that worked alone—especially a female officer—into a potentially volatile situation was not ideal but when a call like this came in, it had to be the closest available vehicle that got dispatched and, this time, that had been Kelly.

She wasn't about to stand back and wait for the back-up of the ambulance that she had heard being dispatched at the same time she had received the Code Red, urgent priority callout, on her radio. Not when there was a pregnant woman and a midwife on scene who needed assistance. She just needed to remember her training. To keep a clear escape route behind her at all times and to carry a heavy bit of kit like the defibrillator in front of her so that, in the worst-case scenario, she could throw it at someone to make her escape easier.

There was a woman leaning on an iron railing fence that separated her property from the house they'd been dispatched to.

''Bout time someone got here,' she told Kelly, with satisfaction. 'He's kicking off again.'

Kelly acknowledged the greeting with no more than a nod. She could hear a raised voice coming from inside the house so she walked past the neighbour and rapped on the open door.

'Ambulance,' she called loudly.

The hallway was empty. The man's angry voice was coming from a room to one side.

'It's her own bloody fault. I reckon she got

pregnant on purpose. How do I even know the kid's mine?'

It was the cry of pain from a woman that made Kelly move, her hackles rising as she got closer to what turned out to be a living room. She held the heavy life pack in front of her body as she'd been trained to do—poised to hurl it if she found herself under attack. The angry man wasn't making an assault on anyone, however. He had a can of beer in his hand and he was simply standing in the doorway to a kitchen. The woman who sounded as if she was in severe pain was lying on a couch and there was another man crouched beside her.

An extraordinary-looking man, with olive brown skin and his hair pulled up into a bun that was a lot higher than the one Kelly always used to tidy her own hair for work. A lot messier, too. He was wearing jeans and a leather jacket of all things but he had what looked like a professional medical kit open on the floor beside him with a stethoscope and blood-pressure cuff visible. And he was placing his hands on the woman's pregnant belly. Large, capable-looking hands, she noticed, but even from this distance she could see—or sense—how gentle his touch was. Kelly wasn't the only one watching.

'Get ya hands off her,' the man yelled. 'Nobody touches my wife without my say so.'

He lunged towards the couch but Kelly was faster as she stepped into the room at the same moment to get between him and the pregnant woman. He stopped in his tracks and swore vehemently but then backed off a little. He was a bully, Kelly realised, lowering the defibrillator. He might thrive on making threats but he was actually unlikely to follow through on them. Not that that made the abuse or interference with medical care any more acceptable, of course.

'It's not my fault,' he muttered as he stepped back. 'It's that cow next door. She's the one who's causing all the trouble round here—not me. So we were having a bit of a barney...so what? Who doesn't?'

'What *is* happening here?' Kelly only took her gaze off him for an instant because, while she thought she had the measure of this man, he was still clearly posing a threat. Her swift glance over her shoulder was long enough to see that the woman on the couch was looking distressed and far too pale. It was also long enough for the man who was crouched beside her to look up and meet her gaze.

Dark, dark eyes. A serious expression on a very intelligent-looking face.

'I'm Kelly,' she introduced herself. 'From the ambulance service.' She was still a little confused about who this man was. 'And you are…?'

'He's a midwife,' the man in front of her sneered. 'A *boy* midwife. And you're a *girly* medic. Who let you out to play all by yourself? If you ask me, the world's gone bloody mad…' He crumpled his beer can, hurled it towards the corner of the room and then turned back towards the kitchen. 'I need another drink…'

Kelly ignored him, her gaze fixed on the midwife. She could sense that, beneath that calm expression, he was worried about his patient. Seriously worried.

'I often work with the obstetric and neonatal flying squad,' she told him. 'Do we need to call them?'

The flying squad was a specialised team with a dedicated ambulance that was mainly used for transport of premature or sick babies to a hospital like the Kensington, which had a neonatal intensive-care unit, but it could also cater for any obstetric emergency like a home birth going wrong or a complication like a post-partum haemorrhage or obstructed labour. The team could include an obstetrician and/or a neonatal specialist, midwives and paramedics and had an incubator as part of their equipment in case an out-of-hospital birth or transport was needed for a fragile infant.

'Maybe.' There was a hint of a smile on his face as the midwife spoke to Kelly for the first time but it was ironic rather than amused. 'For now, it's good that you're a "girly" paramedic. Between us, we might be able to properly assess how much blood Vicky's actually losing.'

Any hint of that smile had faded but his glance still communicated the fact that this man was well aware of the threat that Vicky's husband posed and that his attitude to a male midwife being here was exacerbating that threat. He wasn't about to let it stop him doing his job, which deserved serious respect as far as Kelly was concerned. That simple reference to her being "girly" conveyed both an understanding of the kind of prejudice that could come with crossing perceived career boundaries or trying to assert authority and the kind of humour that meant he'd learned long ago how to deal with it. That earned more than respect from Kelly.

She *liked* this man.

As an advanced paramedic whose expertise had been requested, Kelly was theoretically now in charge of this scene but she wasn't about to ask this midwife to step back if it wasn't necessary. He had looked as though he knew exactly what he was doing when he'd been checking both the position of the baby and how tender or rigid Vicky's abdomen was, and now he was about to move her clothing to check on her blood loss— something they both needed to assess as rapidly as possible.

A split second later, however, he reared back as an open beer can, spewing froth, whistled through the air to narrowly miss his head. Vicky cried out in fear and shrank back against the couch, even as the midwife moved to shield her, and it was in that instant that Kelly knew this woman had been struck in the past.

Maybe they should have waited until they could have taken Vicky out of there and into an ambulance before starting any assessment or treatment but this was most definitely not the time to start thinking about how she could have improved her management of this scene. Abuse of any kind was totally unacceptable and the midwife—who'd come into this situation alone with the sole intention of looking after a vulnerable woman—could have been seriously injured by that can.

With anger driving her muscles, it only took Kelly three steps to get to the other side of the room, although it was long enough for a hole to get punched into a wall. Not that that slowed Kelly down. If anything, she was even more furious as she faced up to the violent thug that Vicky was unfortunately married to.

'*Get in there,*' she shouted, jabbing her finger in the direction of the kitchen. 'If you so much as put a foot back in this room while we're looking after your wife, I'll have the police here so fast you won't know what's hit you. And, believe me, they'll make sure you don't get to cause any more trouble for anyone for a very, *very* long time. Now... *move...*'

Wow...

Ari had his stethoscope in his ears because, having seen the alarming amount of blood Vicky had already lost, it was a matter of urgency to check on the baby's status, but there was no missing the absolute authority in that voice. This paramedic—Kelly—might be blonde, pretty and as "girly" as they came, but she was not about to get messed with and that was exactly the kind of medical back-up he had hoped would arrive. He moved the rounded bell side of his stethoscope to pick up the baby's heartbeat, which was reassuringly rapid and steady…for now.

'Have you been feeling the baby move today, Vicky?'

'Yes.'

'How long ago did the pain start?'

'I dunno. Maybe an hour. Or maybe a bit longer. The fight started because Brendan didn't like what I was making for lunch and he…he…'

Ari lowered his voice, even though the kitchen door had been slammed behind Brendan. He knew that Kelly was coming back to this side of the room and would be able to hear him.

'Did he hit you, Vicky? Is that how the pain started?'

'N-no…he just…shook me a bit, that's all.'

Again, his gaze met that of the paramedic

for a heartbeat. He could see that Kelly, as a frontline member of the emergency services, had seen it all before. He could also see a fierce determination to help a vulnerable mother-to-be. He recognised that determination easily because it was something Ari had lived with himself for almost as long as he could remember. A need to protect and care for those more vulnerable than himself. Especially babies. Including babies that hadn't been born yet and had no idea how tough life could be.

Kelly had her fingers on Vicky's wrist but Ari knew she wouldn't be able to locate a radial pulse because that had been the first thing he'd tried to assess. The tiny frown that appeared between her eyes was confirmation that she'd taken on board the warning that they needed to move fast. An absent radial pulse was an indication that the blood pressure was far too low.

'Vicky?' Kelly's tone was reassuring. 'I'm going to put a mask on you so that we can give you some oxygen. And I'm going to put an IV line into your arm, love. You've lost a bit of blood and we need to give you some fluids to get your blood pressure back up again. Then we're going to get you into hospital. Is that okay with you?'

Vicky nodded wearily, lying back as she closed her eyes, her response no more than a mumbled assent. Kelly must have noticed that Ari was watching her rather intently because she flicked him a sideways glance. One that acknowledged what they both suspected—that Vicky's placenta could be separating from the uterine wall and the amount of blood she was losing could put her into haemorrhagic shock that could be life threatening—both for this young mother and her baby.

There was a question in Kelly's eyes. 'You okay with staying here?' she asked quietly as she opened her backpack and took out an equipment roll. 'Want me to call for police back-up? There's an ambulance on its way but we could try and get Vicky next door in the meantime.'

Ari kept his voice just as low—no more than a murmur that Vicky probably couldn't catch. 'I'd prefer to get her stable before we move her. Her GCS is dropping already. I reckon we can handle this between us…' He tilted his head towards the kitchen door. 'In fact, I think you could handle it all by yourself.'

A brief curl of one side of Kelly's mouth acknowledged the compliment but her nod was an agreement with his preference to stay put and get some fluid resuscitation started. Movement could make the loss of blood more rapid and Vicky's condition could deteriorate rapidly, tipping her into a possibly irreversible state of shock. Kelly had the tourniquet and the foil packet containing an alcohol wipe in her hands, ready to start establishing an intravenous line.

Ari reached for a cannula, peeling back the plastic cover before holding it out for Kelly to take as soon as she cleaned the skin over the vein she'd chosen in Vicky's forearm. In that moment, they became even more of a team than they had when they'd agreed to stay here and try to stabilise their patient's condition.

'Vicky? Sharp scratch, love, but it's only for a second.' She slid the needle in, slid the cannula into place and released the catch on the tourniquet so swiftly and smoothly it looked like a single action.

Impressive.

'There's a bag of zero point nine percent saline in the kit. Top pocket.'

Ari pulled it out. Then he read out the expiry date for her.

'Thanks…' Kelly paused, a finger pressed onto the vein above the small, plastic tube in Vicky's vein as she reached for the Luer plug he'd left beside her knee. 'Sorry… I didn't catch your name.'

'We didn't exactly get the chance for introductions.' Ari was unwinding the giving set to poke the spike into the bag and then run enough fluid through the tubing to remove any air bubbles. 'I'm Ari. Ari Lawson. I'm a midwife attached to Kensington Hospital.' He held the end of the tubing out to Kelly who took it to attach to the Luer plug. With the IV line securely taped, she worked just as swiftly and smoothly to attach ECG electrodes to Vicky's chest and flick the defibrillator into monitoring mode. Almost immediately, an alarm started sounding.

'She's tachycardic,' Kelly noted. 'And look…' She pointed at the screen, where the bizarre shapes of ectopic beats were interrupting a trace that was rapid enough to have tripped the alarm. She silenced the alarm but it seemed like it had triggered a new wave of tension. Chaos, even?

The kitchen door was flung open behind them.

Ari could feel the surge of adrenaline that made every muscle in his body tense as he started to get to his feet. He could sense the same reaction from Kelly as she gathered her inner resources to face whatever new threat might be coming. After what he'd seen earlier, Ari had every confidence that she *could* deal with it but, this time, he was going to be the one in front. Protecting her.

Or maybe he didn't need to. He could hear a commotion coming from the hallway of this small house. Loud shouting that told him that the police *had* apparently responded to the neighbour's call—perhaps because they knew an ambulance officer had been dispatched and might be in need of back-up?

He could also tell that the arriving officers were both male because it felt like the wave of testosterone arrived in this room before they burst in, and although their equipment like telescopic batons, pepper spray and handcuffs were still attached to their belts or stab-proof vests, it felt like they were demanding attention and advertising their ability to enforce authority. Ari found himself turning his glance towards Kelly again. She'd had the authority to command respect without any kind of weapon, hadn't she?

Except…

She looked different now that these male officers had arrived. Okay, her head was probably dipped because she leaning in to try and calm Vicky, who was trying to sit up and pull her oxygen mask off at the same time, but, for a split second, it almost seemed to Ari that Kelly was ducking her head for another reason. Trying not to be seen, even?

'Brendan…' Vicky was still trying to push past Kelly's hands. 'Don't do anything stupid…'

Ari moved to help Kelly keep Vicky still. The last thing they wanted was an increase in the rate at which she was losing blood.

'It's really important that you keep still, sweetheart,' he said. 'We've got this, okay?'

Even if Brendan hadn't been drunk enough to make it difficult to stand up straight, he would have been incapacitated within seconds by the two police officers.

Ari wondered if one of them, in particular, was enjoying the opportunity to use physical force to restrain someone a little too much as he flourished his baton and raised his voice. He was a big man with buzz-cut blond hair that accentuated uncompromising features, including a very square jaw. Kelly was watching as well as the officer twisted Brendan's arm behind him with enough force to make him cry out in pain.

Kelly's expression made Ari suspect that she shared his opinion that too much force was being used here. It certainly looked like her desire to protect an underdog was automatically overriding any desire to remain in the background. She jumped to her feet, although her words were almost tentative.

'H-he hasn't hurt anybody,' she told the police officers. 'He's drunk, that's all. Noisy. He was just…making some verbal threats.'

She was being ignored as the officer issued a rapid, almost bored-sounding caution.

'You do not have to say anything. But it may harm your defence if you do not mention when questioned something which you later rely on in court…'

What Kelly had said wasn't exactly true, Ari thought as he reached for Vicky's wrist to feel for her pulse again. Throwing a full beer can as a weapon was definitely assault. But ambulance staff often got to know local police officers pretty well when they were working in the same area of a city. Was she minimising what had happened here as a form of protection because she knew what this officer might be capable of in the heat of the moment?

Finishing the caution, the big, blond officer pushed Brendan towards his partner and then stepped closer to Kelly. Rather too close in Ari's opinion. Any further and he would have been able to touch her ear with his lips but Ari could still hear what he said.

'You called for us, Cowbell. So why don't you just let us do our thing and look after you, okay?'

Oh, *man*…

How humiliating was this?

Kelly could actually feel the bright flash of colour that was heating her cheeks. She certainly couldn't miss the way Ari's jaw dropped as he heard that patronising tone and the dismissive nickname either. Or the expression in his eyes, even though his gaze only grazed hers for a heartbeat. He didn't understand, did he? He'd seen her stand up to an aggressive, obnoxious drunk with no more than her voice and determination as weapons so why was she letting another bully take charge?

Kelly didn't understand it herself. It was more than two years since her relationship with this man had ended. She should have been over it long ago. She had proved she was strong enough to keep herself completely safe from any other disastrous entanglement. Stupid nicknames should have lost any power long ago as well but, apparently, they could still sting.

Cowbell... Or maybe Kettlebell, because that's all you are, sweetheart. A useless lump...

At least it was chaotic enough for anyone's impressions or embarrassment to be so fleeting that they were unlikely to be remembered. Brendan was being dragged, shouting, from the room at the same moment that paramedics were coming in with a stretcher laden with more equipment. Vicky was crying and another alarm was sounding on the defibrillator. The focus needed on her patient was welcome. Kelly knew that treating a critically ill person was at the top of that list of things she was *not* useless at and she was going to use every one of those skills right now, for the sake of Vicky and her unborn baby.

Vicky's heart rate was climbing. Her blood pressure, oxygen saturation and level of consciousness were dropping. They needed to increase the rate of fluid resuscitation with another IV line. They also needed to get this patient to hospital. Fast.

Only minutes later, Kelly was making sure that all her monitoring equipment for continuous measurements of blood pressure, oxygen saturation and heart rhythm were functioning. One of the back-up paramedics was going to drive her SUV back to the hospital so that she could stay in the ambulance with her patient.

Ari had gathered his own equipment while they'd got Vicky ready for transport. He appeared at the back of the ambulance just before the doors were slammed shut. The flashing lights had already been activated.

'Where are you heading?' he asked.

'Kensington. It's the nearest hospital set up for obstetric and neonatal emergencies.'

'Great. I'm heading that way myself. I'll be able to check up on Vicky later, then.'

Kelly could see him kicking his bike into life and starting to follow them before the ambulance reached the end of the street. She cleared her throat as she received acknowl-edgment from her radio handset that she'd been patched through to Kensington's emergency department.

'We're coming to you with a thirty-seven-year-old woman—Vicky Tomkins,' she told them. 'Pregnant, almost thirty weeks gestation, sudden onset of acute abdominal pain and bleeding approximately ninety minutes ago. Suspected placental abruption. She's on her second unit of saline but her blood pressure's dropped to ninety over forty and her GCS has dropped from fifteen to twelve in the last ten minutes or so. Estimated blood loss of at least a litre. We'll be with you in about six minutes…'

Another glance through the rear window showed Kelly that her rapid response SUV was right behind the ambulance. Just beyond the SUV was a large bike with a tall man in a dark leather jacket and a black helmet.

Ari Lawson—the astonishingly different midwife who had unexpectedly dropped into her life less than an hour ago—was riding shotgun.

For some inexplicable reason that she wasn't going to allow any brain space to analyse, knowing he was close by was making Kelly feel safer. Protected, even.

And it was a good feeling.

CHAPTER TWO

THE FLASHING BLUE lights and the fluorescent red and yellow stripes on the back of the ambulance were easy enough to keep in sight. Weaving his way through the gaps available to a motorbike in the heavy London traffic was so automatic for Ari he was able to think about other things at the same time and, as he noticed the ambulance turning a corner ahead, he was thinking about what was going to happen to Vicky when she arrived at Kensington's emergency department.

He had plenty of background knowledge to draw on. Ari had trained as a nurse before going into midwifery and he had particularly enjoyed his time in Emergency. His fascination with medicine in general continued to fuel his need for further postgraduate study and so far he'd clocked up qualifications in managing high-risk pregnancies and dealing with complications of childbirth and he was currently enrolled in a part-time course on the out-of-hospital care of premature newborns.

By the time he had the ambulance in his line of sight again, having turned the same corner, Ari had decided that Vicky would have as much time as needed in Emergency to support her circulation with aggressive fluid resuscitation and she might be given a blood transfusion as well. If a placental abruption was confirmed, the specialist obstetrician might want to take some fluid from her uterus to reduce the pressure but it was more likely that they would go ahead and deliver the baby by Caesarean section as quickly as possible and then deal with any complications that might follow.

Yvonne would want an update on her client and Ari should have just enough time to duck into the delivery ward on his way to the outpatient department of Kensington's maternity ward where he was due to start an antenatal clinic at three p.m. It was going to be a busy one, with about six women at various stages of pregnancy who needed clinical assessment, any questions answered, reassurance given if needed and advice for the next stage of the journey they were on.

If there was anything abnormal found, he would need to arrange further care and he'd be fielding phone calls as well—from an obstetrician who'd decided to induce a client, perhaps, or from someone who needed to cancel or change an appointment or home visit. Like Yvonne, he could have a client who went into labour unexpectedly and that would throw his schedule into complete chaos, but the prospect didn't bother Ari. He thrived under that kind of pressure and somehow making it work.

Something was bothering him, however, as he had to wait and watch the ambulance go through the red light of an intersection ahead of him. As the emergency vehicle got further ahead, Ari realised what it was that was niggling at the back of his head. Something about Kelly—the paramedic in that ambulance—had got completely under his skin.

He'd been blown away by her courage in subduing an angry, intoxicated man who outweighed her enough to have been dangerous. He'd already felt a beat of connection with her when Brendan had been so dismissive of any authority or skill either of them might have in their chosen professions. The recognition of the kind of determination to protect the vulnerable that, given the right circumstances, could make you much braver than you might think you were or that others might think you were was another connection that tapped into parts of Ari's life that nobody he worked with knew about.

He'd also been seriously impressed with her calm confidence and obvious skill in her job to stabilise a patient whose condition was clearly deteriorating. But—and this was what was really bothering him—the way she'd visibly shrunk into herself when that macho idiot of a cop had turned up. He knew the type. A big ego, a bit of a bully. Capable of making sure the people around him behaved the way *he* wanted them to and to use whatever means necessary to do so.

But Ari had also learned long ago what even the faintest smell of fear was like. He'd seen, all too often, the effects that were the aftermath of trauma, whether it was physical or emotional, and he also knew, all too well, what it was like to feel vulnerable. And he'd been aware of all of that in Kelly's body language when that cop had pushed himself into her personal space and put her down with such biting efficiency.

What had Kelly ever done to provoke that kind of treatment? And calling her *Cowbell*? What the heck was that about? Not that it mattered, anyway. The man had been unprofessional to the point where an official complaint might be justified but that hadn't entered his head at the time. No...the only thing that Ari had wanted to do in that moment was to protect Kelly. The way he would always want to protect someone who was vulnerable and under threat.

The urge had been so powerful that, if Vicky hadn't started crying at that moment, he would have been on his feet and by Kelly's side. Telling that cop just how she had taken control of a situation that had been a lot more threatening than the one he and his colleague had arrived into. And that Kelly had gained control by using nothing more than her voice and her determination. She hadn't needed to wave weapons around or cause physical pain.

His intervention hadn't been required, of course. He might have caught a glimpse of the other side of the coin that was Kelly but it had only been momentary. She'd gone right back to doing her job without her focus being compromised one little bit. Strength had won out over vulnerability. That glimpse had been enough, however. Especially given the connection he was already aware of.

Ari was intrigued.

He wanted to know more.

And, yeah…he knew he should just let it go because that kind of interest had created problems before. He'd never had the space for a woman in his life who wanted to depend on a long-term relationship and he didn't have the space for another woman in his life for any reason right now.

The ambulance carrying Kelly and Vicky was turning into the bay right outside Kensington's emergency department. Ari couldn't park his bike there so he had to go further down the road to access the staff car park. He'd have to walk back this way to head towards the maternity wing, though. Well… okay, it was a bit of a detour and he didn't exactly have the luxury of time to be making detours but…

…but the pull to do that was so strong he knew it might well prove to be irresistible.

* * *

Different.

That was what was so intriguing about Ari the midwife.

It wasn't simply that a male midwife was unusual. Or that he wore his hair long enough to need to tie it back to keep it out of the way for work. It wasn't even the strangely hot contrast between the idea that he had chosen his profession because he loved babies and that obvious gentleness in caring for his clients and the sheer masculinity of a big man who rode around on a powerful motorbike and wore leather.

There was something else that Kelly couldn't quite nail down and, now that she had the time to think about something other than the patient she'd just accompanied to hospital, her brain didn't want to let it go. She was in a supply room down the corridor from the emergency department at Kensington Hospital, collecting everything she needed to restock the kit that was in the back of her rapid response car. The task was automatic. And easy, because all she had to do was run back through the scene in her head and pick up a replacement for everything she'd used.

An oxygen mask was first on the list and

then it was IV supplies. Kelly added a strip of alcohol wipes to the bag, a sixteen-gauge cannula and a couple of Luer plugs and occlusive dressings. She had to stand on tiptoe to reach the shelf with bags of saline and the packages containing the giving sets.

It wasn't just the treatment she had given her patient that Kelly was remembering as she collected the items. She was remembering the assistance she'd had. How easy it had been to work with someone who could anticipate what she needed and when. He was probably quite capable of inserting an IV line himself but he hadn't given the slightest hint of being frustrated at her taking the lead. A lot of men wouldn't like that, especially if that lead was being taken by a woman. Especially men like Darryn...

And there it was...that thing that had been at the back of her mind that felt important enough to identify. The reason that Ari was so different. It was the contrast between those two men that was almost as blinding as the difference between light and dark. Superficially, that contrast was there for everybody to see. Blond and fair-skinned against a Mediterranean kind of colouring. But the difference that Kelly could now see in retrospect was something only she could be aware of and that was the contrast in how those two men made her feel.

It was pathetic, given that she'd escaped her relationship with Darryn so long ago, that he could still make her feel stupid. Belittled. Afraid of what was going to come next, whether it was something being broken or vicious words or the threat of physical harm that seemed just as bad as any actual violence might have been. Worse, in some ways, because there was no evidence left that might have made others realise that something was very wrong. And why would anyone have believed her when he could be so very charming in public? She wouldn't have believed it herself back in the early days when he'd set out to capture her heart. Now it was hard to believe that she could ever have imagined herself to be in love with him.

And in contrast to that was the feeling of...of *safety*...that Ari had given her. She'd only really noticed it when she'd seen him following the ambulance on that huge motorbike but it had been there right from the moment she'd met him, hadn't it? When she'd seen him crouched beside Vicky as she'd entered that living room. There'd been something in his body language that had made her aware of his total focus on the pregnant woman. Something she could sense in the gentle movement of his hands on her belly that had made her think that if *she* was his patient she would feel safe.

She'd seen that look on his face when he'd heard Darryn taunting her with that horrible, old nickname. As unlikely as it seemed, Kelly could believe that he knew exactly how she was feeling in that moment and he'd almost looked as if he was ready to leap to his feet and come to defend her, but maybe she'd imagined that. In any case, it had been Vicky who had needed his attention far more than she had.

Remnants of that feeling of safety were still there, however, and it was doing something weird to Kelly's gut. Making it feel like it did when she was nervous—a fluttering kind of sensation. Stronger than butterflies. More like birds. It wasn't an unpleasant feeling but it was unusual enough for Kelly to prefer that it would go away. Grabbing a handful of ECG electrodes, she headed back to the ambulance bay where her vehicle had been left to one side. She opened the back hatch and then opened her kit to lie flat so that she could slot her replacement supplies into the pouches they belonged in.

The movement and change of scene seemed to have done the trick in dispelling that strange fluttering sensation. Maybe now that she had identified what had been niggling at the back of her mind, she could now dismiss that as well. It wasn't as if she was likely to see Ari again anytime soon and, even if she did, it wouldn't mean anything. So what if he was the polar opposite of her ex-boyfriend? That didn't mean that she was attracted to him, did it? She hadn't been remotely interested in men since she'd broken up with Darryn and that was long enough now to make her think she might remain single for ever.

Zipping her kit closed, Kelly tightened the safety belts that held the defibrillator and an oxygen cylinder in place and then pulled the hatch shut. She was already fishing for the set of keys in her pocket as she turned to see the tall figure walking towards her. The man she hadn't expected to see again anytime soon. If she'd been trying to subconsciously convince herself that those wingbeats in her belly didn't have anything to do with attraction, she realised in that moment that it was a totally lost cause because just the sight of Ari made them spiral into an intensity that was a shaft of something rather too close to physical pain.

The pain of a barrier being smashed, perhaps?

'Hey…just the person I was hoping to see.'

He was smiling at her. She hadn't seen anything more than the hint of a smile on his face before and it was lovely. Warm. Genuine. Enough to make his eyes crinkle at the corners. Brown eyes, she noticed as he came close enough—just as warm as that smile. It was impossible not to smile back.

'All good?' Ari asked. 'How's Vicky? I was hoping to get here sooner but I got held up with some calls.'

'You would have needed to be quick. I was most impressed with how fast they worked. There was a team waiting for us in Resus. An ultrasound confirmed the placental abruption and also revealed that there was quite a lot of blood trapped behind the placenta so what we saw was only part of the volume she'd lost.'

'No wonder she was going into shock. Did she need a transfusion?'

Kelly nodded. 'They had the first unit running as they took her up to Theatre.' She glanced at her watch. 'Her baby should be being delivered right about now. You'll probably be able to see her on one of the maternity wards later this afternoon. I'm just hoping that they'll both be okay.'

'You and me both.' Ari's smile was long gone. 'Especially if she's going back to that violent thug of a husband.'

'The police involvement was part of the ambulance report so Social Services has been notified. If Vicky wants help, it's there for her.'

'I'll put something in my paperwork as well. My colleague, Yvonne, will be doing the postnatal house calls so I'll have a chat to her. I'd hate to have her go back into an abusive relationship.'

'Mmm…' Kelly had to look away from Ari's gaze. It was too intense. As if he really did see more than he should.

'And what about that cop? I'm tempted to put in a complaint about his behaviour.'

Kelly's heart missed a beat. 'What behaviour?'

'Brendan might be a thug but he was handled pretty roughly. And—' there was a note of anger in Ari's voice '—I didn't like the way he spoke to you either.'

Kelly sucked in a quick breath. 'Don't say anything. Please. It would only make things worse.'

'What things?'

'He's my ex,' she admitted. 'It was over a long time ago and we don't cross paths very often but... I wouldn't want to stir things up. You know...'

There was a beat of silence between them. A beat that was so long Kelly had to look back to catch Ari's gaze.

He did know, she thought. More than she would have been prepared to admit to anyone on first acquaintance. But that wasn't stopping him from wanting to know more. What was even stranger was that she wanted to tell him more. To tell him everything, in fact, and maybe she would have said more right then but as she opened her mouth, her pager sounded.

'Uh-oh...' She glanced at the message. 'Code Red. I need to go.'

'Me, too.' Ari stepped out of her way but didn't keep going. 'I finish work about six,' he told her as she opened her car door. 'Want to meet for a drink or a coffee or something?

I might be able to update you on Vicky by then.'

Kelly slammed her door shut but immediately pressed the button that rolled her window down. Already, her focus was veering towards her next callout but that new twist of her gut was sharp enough to make her catch her breath.

'Sure,' she heard herself saying. 'Where?'

'There's a pub on the corner. The Kensington Arms. It's the hospital's local, I believe. See you there at six-thirty?'

Kelly was putting her vehicle into reverse. She flicked a switch to start the beacons on her roof. She could actually feel her adrenaline levels rising. Excitement at not knowing what she was being dispatched to this time? Or did it also have something to do with the prospect of meeting Ari again? Outside work hours. Almost like a date…

'I'll be there,' she told him. Her vehicle was pointing the right way now and her foot was poised over the accelerator. She caught his gaze for a heartbeat, however. She couldn't quite find a smile because this suddenly seemed a little overwhelming and she put her foot down as she spoke, as if she needed to escape. 'See you then.'

* * *

"Intrigued" didn't quite cover how Ari was feeling about Kelly by late that afternoon.

He should have known there was a reason why he'd felt such a strong urge to protect her when that cop had demonstrated that he had absolutely no respect for her personal space. An ex-boyfriend? What on earth had she ever seen in him? And if he could treat her like that in public, well after the relationship had ended, what had he been like when they had been together, behind closed doors?

Unfortunately, Ari could imagine only too well and he was sure he was right in his suspicions. Kelly was an intelligent, capable, gorgeous-looking woman and there was only one thing that could have undermined her self-esteem enough to make her personality visibly shrink in front of him like that and that was abuse. Pure and simple. He'd not only seen it too many times in his life not to recognise the signs, he knew what it was like to be on the receiving end. He'd only just met Kelly but he could feel anger on her behalf. And sadness. And…the desire to try and help her.

Just as a friend, of course, because no matter how undeniably attractive she was that was all he could offer, but that might be enough to make her believe in how amazing she was. To help heal whatever damage that bastard had done to her and let her move forward with her life with the kind of confidence that would make sure nobody could ever put her down like that again—in public or in private.

The thought had to be shelved as his last appointment for this antenatal clinic came into the room, a small sample container in her hand.

'Sorry that took so long. I couldn't do much either.'

'Doesn't need much for a dipstick test.' Ari unscrewed the jar on his desk and took out the test strip to dip into the urine sample. He compared the colours in the tiny squares to the chart on the jar.

'It's all good, isn't it?'

'Your protein level's up a fraction. We'll need to keep an eye on that. I might get a culture done to make sure you're not brewing up a urinary tract infection.'

'That's dangerous for the baby, isn't it? I'm sure I read something about protein in urine being bad.'

'If it's there along with high blood pressure, it can be a sign of something called pre-eclampsia and that can be dangerous if it's not recognised in time. But your blood pressure's fine, Janice.' He smiled at her. 'Try not to worry so much.'

'I can't help it. We've waited a long time for this baby, you know?'

'I know. But you're well past the halfway mark now and everything's looking great. Come and hop up on the bed and I'll measure your tummy and we can listen to baby's heartbeat. We can have a chat about whether you want to start making a birth plan as well.'

'Oh…yes… I've been thinking about that a lot. I've even chosen the music I want.'

Ari grinned. 'Maybe we could choose the place you want to give birth as a first step. You were considering a home birth, weren't you?'

'I've gone right off that idea.' Janice lay back on the bed and pulled down the waistband of her maternity jeans to expose her bump. 'What if something went wrong? I'd rather be somewhere safe that had all the experts and medical stuff that I might need.'

'Safety is certainly my number one priority,' Ari agreed. 'For both you and your baby.'

He had his handheld Doppler ready, holding the monitor in one hand and the small transducer in the other, pressing it gently to one side of Janice's bump as he searched for the best place to hear the baby's heartbeat. It took a few seconds for the faint thumping sounds to become clearer.

'There we go.' Ari turned the monitor so that Janice could see the readout. 'One forty beats per minute. Perfect.'

Janice was smiling but her lips wobbled a moment later. 'It gets me every time, hearing that,' she admitted.

Ari had to smile back. 'Me, too.'

The miracle of new life never got old. The emotions that went with it covered every human experience from anguish to ecstasy and, as Ari chatted to Janice about making her birth plan, he hoped that her experience was going to be as joyful as possible. Some women never had the luxury of any control over how their babies came into the world— like poor Vicky today. Ari had half an eye on the clock on his wall. He wanted to get an update on how Vicky and her baby were doing because Kelly would want to know and he would be seeing her very soon.

If that little Doppler had been anywhere near his own heart right now, it would have picked up that little blip of a missed beat as well as the acceleration that followed. Anticipation, that's what it was. He was very much looking forward to seeing her again.

'Let's wrap this up for today, Janice. I've got a printout here of all the things you can think about and talk to your partner about. Like pain relief options, what kind of food and drink you might want available in labour, preferred positions or use of water. Even who gets to cut the cord. There's lots to think about.'

'There sure is.' Janice's eyes had widened. 'Thanks, Ari. Do I need to make another appointment?'

'Yes.' Ari opened his diary. 'And I'll be in touch about the results of any further testing on your urine sample. If necessary, I'll refer you to your GP for a blood test or any medication you might need.'

Minutes later, Ari stripped off the scrub top he'd been wearing to replace it with a black T-shirt and then his leather jacket. He collected his satchel from the corner of the room but didn't bother picking up his motor-bike helmet. He could walk to the Kensington Arms and come back for the helmet later.

The sound of an incoming text message as he turned towards the door was nothing to worry about. They were almost always about an appointment that needed to be changed. People always rang rather than texted if it was something urgent. Except that this message was something different. Nothing to do with his work and everything to do with what currently had such a high priority in his life.

He read the message and then hit a rapid dial key.

'What's happening, Peggy?' He listened for only a matter of seconds, a frown deepening rapidly on his face. 'Okay,' he interrupted. 'It's okay. I'll be there as soon as I can.'

He had to pick up his helmet and he was walking fast through the corridors of the maternity wing. He still had his phone in his hand, ready to call or text Kelly to let her know he couldn't make it. But…he hadn't asked for her number, had he? He had no way of contacting her because he certainly didn't have either the time or the head space to start searching for and ringing around all the ambulance stations on this side of town. Or to go to find someone who might know her contact details because of her involvement in the flying squad. It would have to wait until later.

Ari could only hope that she would understand but if she didn't that would be just the way things had to be. This was why he'd come back here. To be able to provide support for someone who needed him. The only woman in his life that he'd ever been able to trust completely, in fact, and that was why she deserved everything he could give her at the moment. It was also why he didn't have space in his life for anyone else right now, possibly even a new friend.

'What can I get you, love?'

Kelly smiled at the bartender, who had a strong Aussie accent. 'I'll wait, thanks. I've got a friend coming.' She glanced sideways at the huge railway clock on the wall. She was a few minutes late herself so she had no right to feel disappointed that Ari wasn't here already.

'No worries.' The bartender grinned at her. 'Lucky guy.'

Kelly shook her head. 'It's nothing like that. He's just a friend.'

Not even that, really. Or not yet. But the possibility was there. Of friendship. Of possibly—okay, a very small possibility but it had to be acknowledged—something more than friendship.

And there were parts of Kelly's body that felt like they were waking up after a very long hibernation. Tingly bits that were not at all unpleasant. Quite the opposite.

The bar was quite crowded and noisy and Kelly was happy to sit on the bar stool and just relax in the convivial ambience as she let herself contemplate that tingle that had resurfaced at quite frequent intervals over the last few hours. It wasn't freaking her out any more. In fact, she had identified something she hadn't felt in so long it was almost a new concept in regard to her personal life.

Hope…that's what it was…

The bartender went past, his hands filled with empty glasses. 'Sure you don't want something while you're waiting?'

Blinking out of that daydream, Kelly looked at the clock and was astonished to find another fifteen minutes had gone by. Still, she shook her head, although her smile was harder to find this time. The atmosphere didn't feel so friendly after that either. Had people noticed her sitting here alone? Was some of that laughter on her account? Oh, God…maybe some of Darryn's mates were in here and talking about her. Passing on those nicknames and a warning to stay clear of someone who was too stupid to live.

Had she really thought that being around Ari the midwife made her feel safer? Well… that trust had been totally misplaced, hadn't it? Right now, sliding off the bar stool, Kelly felt just as humiliated as she had when Darryn had reminded her of how worthless he thought she was.

She'd been stood up. Nobody did that to someone they had the slightest respect for, did they?

Not that she should feel this surprised. Or hurt. She knew better than to trust any man. Even one with soft, dark eyes that told her they could understand. That they wanted to know her story. That they thought she was something special.

Kelly's breath came out in an incredulous huff as she let the pub door swing shut behind her. Who was she trying to kid? They were *especially* the kind of men you couldn't trust. The ones who got under your guard and sucked you in so fast they made you feel things that you thought you'd forgotten how to feel. Maybe even feeling those things wasn't worth it, because when reality came along and smacked you in the face, it really sucked.

'Hey…you're going the wrong way, darlin'.' A group of young men were heading into the pub but one of them had turned back. 'Come and have a drink with us, why don't you?'

Kelly shook her head. And walked faster. There was only one place she wanted to be and that was her little basement flat where she lived alone. Where she had only herself to rely on.

Where she felt genuinely safe…

CHAPTER THREE

Code Red... Suspected opioid overdose.
Seventeen-year-old female who can't be
woken. Pregnant...unknown gestation...

KELLY HIT THE switches for both the lights
and siren on her SUV and put her foot down
as she moved into a bus lane to get past the
queued traffic at the intersection. The address wasn't far away so she was already
planning what to take into the scene and how
to handle what was an all too common callout.

Looking for the signs and symptoms of
an opioid overdose was a well-practised
routine. Pinpoint pupils, cold, clammy skin,
slow heart rate and, if more serious, cyano-
sis with blue lips or nails and respiratory distress that was enough to be causing gurgling
or even no breathing at all so Kelly needed

to be prepared to deal with a cardiac arrest on her own until an ambulance could be dispatched to back her up.

Her radio crackled into life.

'Control to Rover One.'

'Rover One receiving, go ahead.'

'Back-up from ambulance fifteen minutes away. Do you want a police unit dispatched?'

'Ah...' Kelly thought fast. The treatment for an overdose of this sort was straightforward with a dose of Narcan almost guaranteed to rapidly reverse the effects of the drugs taken. It also put the patient into withdrawal, however, and this could often cause a degree of agitation that put medics in danger of injury, perhaps from a flying fist.

A tiny flash of memory was so lightning fast it didn't interfere at all with Kelly's thought processes but it still managed to generate a knot in her stomach. She'd coped with the threat of violence only yesterday from someone far more threatening than a pregnant seventeen-year-old girl probably was. Mind you, she hadn't been alone and maybe she'd been braver than she might have otherwise been because Ari the midwife had been in the room and she'd known she had back-up. But, in reality, she *had* been alone—

because Ari the midwife wasn't as trustworthy as she'd thought, was he?

That pang of disappointment hadn't faded much overnight, had it? Kelly could feel every muscle in her body tensing as she pushed the unwanted emotion away. It helped enormously that the adrenaline from travelling towards the unknown with her lights and siren on was kicking in.

'Negative, thanks, Control,' she said. 'I'll assess the scene and let you know what I need in the way of any back-up.'

Even an ambulance to transport the patient to hospital was not necessarily going to be needed and, in fact, could tie up a lot of time and emergency services resources if the patient didn't want to co-operate. The main danger of reversing an overdose and then releasing the patient from care was potentially fatal rebound opioid toxicity when the effects of the reversal drug were wearing off, although recent research suggested that was extremely unlikely if the patient had normal vital signs and level of consciousness.

The fact that this patient was pregnant might tip the balance for making that decision for Kelly, however. It could influence whether she gave the drug in the first place, in fact, because giving any drug in pregnancy was only indicated if really needed and where the benefit outweighed any risks. She'd also need to find out whether this girl was getting antenatal care and she might need to contact her general practitioner or midwife if she had one.

And there it was again…an unwelcome reminder of yesterday's case. Of a meeting that had been not just memorable for it being a male midwife but because he had been a man who had both sparked and then crushed a glimmer of restored faith in the opposite sex. The opportunity for Kelly to use her air horn and blast a car that was refusing to pull aside to let her past was a rather welcome way to clear her head and dismiss what had happened yesterday. It was highly unlikely that a pregnant teenager who was a drug taker would have a midwife, anyway. It was far more likely that Kelly would need to activate back-up from Social Services.

Today was a new start and, as always, Kelly's complete focus was on the job she loved. She shut down her siren as her satnav told her she was almost at her destination and then killed the beacons as she slowed down to find the street number. It looked like it was that rather nice, rambling old house on the edge of a park, which was a little unexpected. Many calls like this came from deserted buildings being used by street kids or homeless people. Or had a resident found someone in the park behind the house? Kelly put her backpack on and picked up both the defibrillator and an oxygen cylinder.

There was no answer to her knock on the door, so Kelly tried the doorknob and found it unlocked. She stepped into a hallway.

'Ambulance,' she called. 'Where are you?'

'In here…'

The voice was that of an older woman—a little frail and quiet—but it was enough to direct Kelly to a room off the right side of a hallway. A bedroom that had a figure curled up with a duvet covering her body and another person sitting on the end of the bed.

'I'm Kelly, from the ambulance service.' Kelly put her gear down near the head of the bed. She was already assessing the girl lying there and she knew this wasn't an emergency. The patient she'd been called to see seemed to be breathing quite normally and her skin was a good colour. The teenager opened her eyes to glare at Kelly as she reached to take her pulse, pulled her hand away and rolled over with a muttered curse.

'I couldn't wake her up before,' the elderly woman told Kelly. 'And…and I couldn't find my patches… I got scared…'

Kelly nodded as she pushed the button on her radio. 'Rover One to Control.'

'Control receiving, go ahead, Rover One.'

'On scene. No back-up required at this stage, thanks.'

'Roger that.'

Kelly clipped her radio back to her belt and turned to crouch a little so that she was on the same level as the silver-haired woman who looked to be in her eighties. 'What's your name?' she asked.

'Peggy. Peggy Hammond. And that's Stacey in bed. She just turned up on the doorstep yesterday. We haven't seen her in years…'

'Okay…' Kelly didn't understand what was going on here but there was more to it than an unhappy, pregnant teenager who didn't want to get out of bed. Peggy looked beyond frail. She was very pale and her fingers were gripping the corner of the duvet as if she was afraid of falling. 'Your patches, Peggy…what are they?'

'Fentanyl.'

'You're in pain?'

Peggy nodded. 'I've got cancer, lovey,' she said softly. 'But don't you worry about me. It's Stacey who needs help.'

'No, I don't.' The mutter from beneath the duvet was sullen. 'I just need some sleep. I'm tired, that's all. I didn't take your stupid patches. I told you I don't *do* drugs any more.'

Kelly's priorities had just changed. 'I can give you something for the pain, Peggy. Can I contact your GP and arrange a visit as well?'

'No…no, I don't want to bother her. I'll be fine. I've called my boy and he'll be here any minute. I'm lucky he wasn't too busy at work at the moment. He's come back to London specially, you know…just to help look after me.'

'That's wonderful.' Kelly couldn't help returning the sweet smile she was receiving. 'How many children have you got, Peggy?'

'Dozens,' came the surprising response. 'But I didn't give birth to any of them. Ironic, isn't it? I was a midwife and I delivered hundreds of babies but could never have one of my own. So I started fostering instead. I could never turn a baby away.'

'That's an amazing thing to have done

with your life.' Kelly could feel a squeeze in her chest that could easily bring tears to her eyes. 'So Stacey is one of the children you fostered?'

'The last baby.' Peggy nodded.

'Stop talking about me,' Stacey snapped. 'Go away.'

Peggy ignored the command. 'I was nearly seventy then,' she told Kelly. 'I couldn't have managed if I hadn't had a lot of help from my oldest boy. He loved the babies, too. Do you know, the first time I ever saw him smiling was when he'd managed to stop a baby crying. *Oh*…' She doubled over as she gasped in agony.

Something like a sob came from under the duvet. 'Shut *up*,' Stacey shouted. 'And go away. Why can't you just go and die somewhere else?'

There was a sudden, shocked silence in the room. And then, as Kelly got to her feet to help, reaching out to hold Peggy's shoulders so that she didn't slip to the floor, the sound of heavy, rapid footsteps could be heard on the wooden floorboards of the hallway. A figure appeared in the doorway. A very tall figure that was even more of a shock to Kelly than the teenaged Stacey's cruel words.

Oh, my God… Of all people… What on earth was *Ari* doing here?

He looked just as shocked to see her. Or perhaps he'd heard what Stacey had shouted but his focus was instantly on Peggy. Kelly had to back away as he crouched in front of Peggy and put his hands on her arms.

'How bad is it, Ma? Have you got a new patch on? Taken a pill to top up?'

'I couldn't find them, love. I thought… I thought Stacey had taken them. She wouldn't wake up and tell me…'

'I was *tired*,' Stacey shouted. 'Why wouldn't I be when Ari kept me up half the night nagging me about baby stuff?'

Kelly's breath caught as she watched how gently Ari was scooping Peggy into his arms.

'We hid your medicine in the biscuit tin last night,' he told her. 'When Stacey was having a bath. Did you remember that?'

'Oh…*no*…' Peggy's frail arms were wrapped around Ari's neck as he lifted her. 'I forgot…'

She looked so small and even more frail in his arms. When she laid her head against his chest with an almost inaudible sigh, Kelly actually had to blink back tears. She could feel the love between these two people and it was powerful enough for her to be caught in the glow. She'd never had someone who cared for her that much in her entire life. Her parents had been loving enough but distant. In the early days, boyfriends had seemed only interested in sex and more recently Darryn had been the final—and worst—of a series of disasters. To be held like that—to be able to let your breath go and relax, as if you had absolute trust that you were safe—how lucky was Peggy?

'I told you I didn't take them.' Stacey's head came out from under the covers. 'I told you I *wouldn't* take them but you didn't believe me, did you? I hate you. I hate *both* of you. I don't know why I came back here.'

'Yes, you do, Stace.' Ari's tone was calm. 'You were living on the streets and you had nowhere else to go and you knew it was the right thing to do to come and ask for help. I'm just going to get Mum sorted and then I'll come back and talk to you, okay?'

'Suit yourself.' Stacey pulled the duvet over her head again. 'Just don't expect *me* to listen to you preaching.'

Kelly stared at the shape beneath the bedding. She still had no idea of Stacey's medical history or stage of pregnancy and hadn't even recorded a single vital sign but she could be sure that there was no medical emergency to be dealt with in this room. Silently, she picked up her gear and followed Ari, hoping that he would let her help with Peggy's care.

Part of her heart was breaking for what was going on in this household. A woman who was facing the end of a life devoted to babies and children who didn't have the safety of a loving family. A teenaged girl, who had obviously struggled with drugs in the past, had been living on the streets and was nowhere near ready to become a mother. A man who could show such love for others simply by the way he touched them or the patience that coated his words to someone who wasn't ready to listen.

Was Ari Peggy's oldest boy? The one who'd smiled for the first time because he'd managed to comfort a baby? Kelly was sure that he was. She was also sure that her first instincts about this man had been correct. Despite the way she'd been let down yesterday, he was trustworthy. More than that. He was someone very different.

Special…

So his priorities yesterday had been to be

with his family instead of meeting someone for a drink at a pub? She had to respect that. It fitted right in with the impression of this man that she'd had from the first moment she'd laid eyes on him and the least she could do was offer any medical skills or access to other resources that might make the challenges Ari was facing a little more bearable.

At the end of the hallway, a kitchen living area spanned the width of this old house. There was a big, scrubbed wooden table that looked like it had hosted countless family dinners, an old dresser cluttered with crockery and a massive corkboard on a wall that had so many photographs pinned to it that some were almost hidden. French doors at one end led out to a garden and inside there was a huge, battered old couch draped with colourful blankets made out of knitted and crocheted squares.

Peggy squares, Kelly thought, a smile tilting her lips as she watched Ari put his foster mother down, oh, so carefully, on the cushions of the couch. Woollen squares that were handmade and as genuine and welcoming as everything else in a room that was very much the heart of a house. Strictly speaking, Peggy was not her patient and she should probably be contacting the ambulance service's control centre to make herself and her vehicle available again for what could be deemed more of an emergency but she didn't want to leave. It wasn't just that she wanted to help in her professional capacity.

This felt personal. And important.

She did radio through to Control, however.

'I'll be on scene for a while longer,' she told them. 'I have a patient here who needs acute pain management.'

'Is transport required?'

Kelly caught Ari's gaze as he shook his head. Then she saw the tears rolling down Peggy's wrinkled cheeks and the flash of something like despair in the elderly woman's eyes.

'Negative,' she said. 'I'll let you know as soon as I'm available.'

Stacey had done everyone a favour, Ari decided as he watched the care Kelly was taking not to bruise Peggy's hand as she slipped a needle through thin, papery skin into one of those prominent veins.

'It's just going to be so much quicker to give you some intravenous morphine,' she was saying. 'A new patch will take quite a while to be effective and even your pills will have trouble getting on top of this pain quickly now that it's got a bit out of control. You've had morphine before, haven't you?'

'Oh, yes, lovey. Too many times now.'

'Mum was diagnosed with ovarian cancer a few months ago,' Ari told Kelly. 'She's just finished a course of chemo intended to shrink the tumour enough to have surgery, including a full hysterectomy.' He held out the peeled-back package containing the Luer plug for Kelly to screw to the end of the cannula. He had the strips of sticky tape to secure the venous access ready as well. 'Do you want a dressing to go on top of that?'

Kelly shook her head. 'I won't leave the IV in. Not if Peggy's going to stay at home.'

'Of course I'm going to stay at home.' There was a fierce determination in Peggy's voice. 'Stacey needs me.'

'Stacey needs more help than you or I can give her right now, Mum. Like I said last night, you've got to look after yourself right now. You were supposed to be admitted today and now your surgery's going to be put back.'

'It's not as if it's going to cure me. We both know that.'

'It's going to buy you time. Maybe more time than you think. You'll be able to do more for Stace by being around for longer. And for all your other kids. Someone else will be landing on the doorstep before too long. They always do.'

Ari wanted her around for as long as possible as well. He wasn't ready to lose the only woman who'd ever been a real mother to him. The only woman he'd ever completely trusted in his life.

Kelly was holding a syringe up in front of her face, having drawn up the morphine and added saline to dilute the drug. She pushed enough to make a fine spray in the air and remove any air bubbles and then took the needle off to screw the syringe to the plug port. She drew back until she could see blood in the chamber, to confirm that the cannula was still patent, and then slowly injected half the dose of morphine in the syringe.

'You'll might feel a bit woozy,' she told Peggy.

'Mmm… Feels like I've had a big drink of gin.'

Ari smiled. 'That was always your favourite, wasn't it? A gin and tonic on a Saturday night.'

'How's the pain now?' Kelly asked. 'What score would you give it if it was ten out of ten before?'

'About five,' Peggy said.

'We'll give it a few minutes and then I'll give you the rest if you need it.' She looked up at Ari. 'Are you going to be home for a while?'

'As long as I can. I've got a client in the early stages of labour so I'll have to go as soon as she needs me.'

'Ari's a midwife,' Peggy told Kelly. 'Just like I was.'

'I know.' Kelly was smiling. 'I met him yesterday. Bit of a coincidence, isn't it?'

'Did you?' Peggy's face had brightened considerably now that she was in less pain but she was a little drowsy. 'Why didn't he tell me that?' She was smiling as her eyes drifted shut. 'It's about time he met a nice girl like you.'

'It was work, Mum,' Ari said. 'Kelly came to help with a young woman who was having a placental abruption and needed to go to hospital. She was in a bit of trouble.'

But it had had the potential to have been more than simply a professional meeting.

What would have happened if he'd turned up for that drink, like they'd arranged?

'I'm sorry,' he told Kelly quietly.

She was wrapping a blood pressure cuff around Peggy's arm. 'What for?'

'That I didn't make it to the pub. When I heard that Stace had turned up, I had to get home.'

'Of course. I understand completely.' Kelly lifted her gaze as she unhooked her stethoscope from around her neck and fitted the ear pieces.

He knew she had blue eyes. He'd noticed them yesterday as part of that classic combination with her blonde hair. He hadn't noticed quite how dark they were, however, or was it sincerity that was adding that depth of colour? She really *did* understand, didn't she?

'I was kicking myself that I didn't ask you for your number,' he added. 'I was doing something about that this morning, so I could contact you and apologise for standing you up like that.'

'It's okay. No big deal.' Kelly opened the valve to deflate the cuff. 'Blood pressure's down a bit but the systolic's still well over a hundred. We can top that morphine up if necessary.' She threw a quick smile in Ari's direction. 'I've already forgiven you anyway.'

'Just as well.' If Kelly hadn't turned away to reach for Peggy's wrist, he might have got caught staring at her face for too long but who wouldn't, with a smile like that on offer? 'I found one of the doctors from the obstetric and neonatal flying squad but he wouldn't give me your contact details. He said personal information was only available for team members. He also said they could do with another midwife on the team if I was interested.'

'Oh? And are you? Interested?'

Kelly looked as if she might welcome his presence on a team she belonged to but Ari shook his head. 'I spent time with a similar unit in Glasgow and loved it but…that's not why I'm back in London.'

Peggy opened her eyes. 'Ari gave up his job,' she told Kelly. 'Just to come back to London so he could help look after me. I told him he had to have his work as well, though. It's lovely to have him around but I can look after myself. Besides…' There was a twinkle in her eyes now. 'I like hearing the work stories. Takes me right back, it does. I'd have loved to have been on one of those flying squads. You should do it, Ari. You've got a special gift that you should be using, instead of spending your days off looking after a sick, old lady.'

'You're my mum,' Ari told her. 'End of story. Maybe I'll think about it after things settle down around here.'

'And when hasn't life been messy in this house?' Peggy patted his hand but it was Kelly she turned to. 'I didn't normally take older children,' she said. 'But little Ari came along when he was about six or seven and I just couldn't resist. And he just stayed and stayed. By the time he was a teenager I couldn't have managed without him. He was the man of the house. And a...what do they call them these days? Those people who have the magic touch with babies?'

'A baby whisperer?' Kelly was biting her lip, as if she was really amused.

'That's the one.' Peggy was smiling now. 'Poor wee Stacey was only a few weeks old and she was still going through withdrawal when she came here. Her mum was an addict. Never heard a baby cry so much.' She turned her gaze back to Ari. 'She was hard work, wasn't she, love?'

'Still is,' Ari murmured. 'I need to go and

talk to her. I'm expecting a call back from her case worker at Social Services. We'll be making a plan.'

'She doesn't need a plan. She can stay here until she has the baby.'

'With all your drugs in the house? When she's only been clean for a few months, if that?' Ari shook his head. 'And I heard what she said to you before. That's not the kind of thing you should have to put up with.'

Kelly obviously agreed with him, judging by the look on her face. Yeah… He already knew that she knew how damaging cruel words could be. Ari could feel a beat of that pull towards Kelly that he'd been so aware of yesterday. That vulnerability hiding beneath such a strong exterior that he wanted to know more about.

'She's upset,' Peggy said softly. 'She came here needing help and found that *I* was one who's needing help now. She's cross, that's all. She's only seventeen, remember. And she's got some big decisions to make about that baby or hers.' Trying to sit up, Peggy visibly winced.

'You're still pretty sore, aren't you?' Kelly glanced at her watch. 'I'm going to give you the rest of this morphine. If you're still in too much pain in another ten minutes, it might be worth considering a trip to hospital to really get on top of it.'

Ari nodded. 'They might even let you keep your surgery slot. The sooner you have that done, the less likely you are to even have this level of pain.'

But Peggy shook her head firmly. 'I'm not going anywhere,' she said. 'Not while Stacey needs me.'

'You know what?' Ari sighed. 'You're stubborn, that's what you are.'

'Look who's talking. Tell you what, Ari. You go and sign up for that flying squad so you can do something you'd love and I'll go and have that operation.'

'You mean that?'

Peggy nodded. 'I'll have Stacey here to help look after me when I get out.'

Ari saw the way Kelly's eyes widened at that suggestion but he'd learned long ago that Peggy's instincts were usually correct.

'Okay…how's the pain now?' Kelly asked.

'So much better. I can move.' Peggy sat up to demonstrate. 'I don't need to go to hospital.' She looked up at Ari. 'So, is it a deal?'

'Is what a deal?'

'You join the flying squad and I'll go and

have that operation as soon as they give me a new date.'

'It's a deal.' Ari would work out how to care for Peggy if Stacey wasn't around by then.

It was Kelly's hand that Peggy patted this time. 'He would have joined anyway,' she said in a stage whisper. 'That way, he gets a chance to get to know you properly. You're just the sort of girl who'd be perfect for my Ari.'

Kelly made a slightly strangled sound but then cleared her throat. 'Let me take this IV out, Peggy. And then you'll need to press on it firmly for a few minutes to stop any bleeding. I'm going to have to get back to work now.'

There was a pink flush to Kelly's cheeks that hadn't been there a minute ago. And it felt like she was avoiding looking at him but Ari didn't get the feeling that she was too embarrassed by Peggy's comments. If she had been, she wouldn't have paused when he was seeing her to the door a couple of minutes later. And she certainly wouldn't have offered to give him her phone number.

'In case you do sign up for the squad,' she

said. 'I can give you a few tips on how it all works.'

'I'll have to sign up now, won't I?' Ari opened his phone to input the number. 'Once Peggy's settled on a bargaining chip, she's not likely to give it up before she gets what she wants.'

Kelly's smile lit up her face when she finished giving him the number. 'She's a bit of a character, your mum.'

Ari's smile felt a little wobbly round the edges. 'She's the best.'

Kelly lowered her voice as she glanced at the bedroom door behind him. 'Good luck,' she murmured. 'I could also steer you in the direction of some organisations that might be able to help if you need support.'

It sounded like Kelly actually wanted him to call her. Was the fact that they could be considered professional rather than personal reasons just a disguise? Ari wasn't blind. He could see that flicker of interest in her eyes. Or maybe he was feeling that connection getting stronger between them. So strong, it was tempting to keep following Kelly towards the front door, just so he could keep her in sight a little longer. But the tiny sound from the bedroom behind him reminded Ari of exactly why he couldn't do that.

'Thanks,' he said. 'I'll keep that in mind. See you around, Kelly.'

He turned back then, and kept moving till he was beside the shapeless lump that was Stacey bundled beneath the duvet.

'Okay, Stace. Are you going to tell me why you're acting up? Is Mum right? Are you angry that she's not well enough to look after you?'

'It's not that she's "not well".' Spiky red hair appeared above huge brown eyes. 'She's *dying*, Ari. And that means I don't have anybody.' She burst into tears as Ari sat on the bed beside her and wrapped his arms around her.

'I know,' he said. 'It's horrible. And it's hard. But she needs our help, Stace. And, hey…you've got me, haven't you? I'm not nobody.'

He'd felt like it once, though, hadn't he? When he'd been a small boy that nobody wanted. When the world had seemed huge and terrifying and he'd been deemed worthless. Until Peggy had wrapped her arms around him, like he was doing for Stacey right now. Until he'd had the love and support that meant he could find his place in the world and follow his passion for helping others in the same way he'd been helped.

It was a foster sister who was half his age that he was focusing on at this moment but he couldn't quite dismiss that thought that was insisting on lingering at the back of his head.

Who loved Kelly enough to provide that kind of support? He had to wonder if she even had anybody at all, if verbal abuse from an ex-partner could make her shrink into herself as if she'd been physically assaulted. At the very least, surely that was something he should find out? Something he needed to find out to give himself some peace of mind. Because nobody should ever be left alone like that, even if it was their choice to keep their secrets and push others away.

Sometimes, just knowing that someone else understood—that you weren't alone—could be enough. And there was no excuse not to find the time to do that.

CHAPTER FOUR

THE SMALL SEMINAR room in Kensington Hospital's maternity wing was full of new faces, which was only to be expected when this was an introductory meeting for volunteers who wanted to be involved with the obstetric and neonatal flying squad service. Kelly recognised a few of them. One was someone she'd worked with at her last ambulance station and another was an emergency department nurse.

And then, of course, there was Ari, who was following through with his promise to his foster mother. Kelly could just imagine the smile on Peggy's face when he'd told her where he was going this evening. She had probably had a very similar smile on her own face when she'd seen him walk through the door because seeing him again just made her feel good. Happy… He was now sitting in the top row of this tiered room, whilst Kelly was down at the front with an obstetric consultant, Phillip Jones, who had just introduced himself.

'Kensington Hospital has the distinction of being one of the first hospitals south of the Scottish border to form and maintain an obstetric flying squad to provide emergency back-up to GPs, ambulances and midwives.'

Kelly's glance shifted back to the only midwife she knew to be in the audience this evening. It had been nearly a week since the call that, in retrospect, may well have changed her life. If she hadn't met Ari again under those very particular circumstances, she would probably have never spoken to him again. She might have dismissed him, like pretty much every man she'd met in the last couple of years, as being untrustworthy and to be avoided at all costs. Not only had she been deeply touched by the closeness of his relationship with Peggy, she'd done something that would have been unthinkable even a week or two ago. She'd given her phone number to a man she'd only just met. She'd even given him a reason to contact her and Ari had done just that, messaging her only a couple of days later.

What do I need to know about signing up for the flying squad?

Your timing is perfect. There's going to be an introductory session for new team members on Thursday night if you're free.

I'll do my best to be there.

His best obviously hadn't been sabotaged by any domestic crisis this time and it was a little disturbing how Kelly's heart had lifted at the sight of him arriving. Her breath had actually caught in her throat when he'd smiled at her. Even now, having had time to give herself a small lecture about the dangers of trusting anyone too much or too fast, finding him watching her so that their gazes caught for a heartbeat was enough to give her a tiny ripple of sensation deep in her abdomen.

Attraction…that's what it was. Mixed with perhaps more than a dollop of hope…

'Our ambulance service does an amazing job…' Phillip gestured towards Kelly, who tilted her head in acknowledgment of the compliment '…but, like a specialist trauma retrieval team, our purpose is manage serious emergencies on scene and to stabilise both the mother and baby so that they can be safely transported to a hospital such as

Kensington that is equipped with adult, neonatal and paediatric intensive care facilities. Because we are a leading tertiary centre in this field, our flying squad is also used as a retrieval service to transport premature or sick babies from other hospitals.'

Kelly had heard all this before. Many times, in fact, so it was no wonder that her attention was slipping a little. Had Peggy been given a new date for her surgery? And what about Stacey? Had she had some antenatal assessment? How far along was she in her pregnancy? Was she still in that big old house with Peggy and Ari? What was going to happen after her baby was born?

So many questions and they barely scratched the surface of what Kelly wanted to know because the answers wouldn't tell her anything more about Ari. Why had he had to go into foster care in the first place? How had he turned out to be as caring and gentle as he obviously was when a lot of children with a similar start in life ended up going in a completely different and destructive direction?

And…did he have anyone else significant in his life? Like a girlfriend?

Kelly could feel her gaze being pulled

back in Ari's direction again but she resisted, keeping it firmly on the man who was still speaking.

'The difference between our flying squad and a trauma retrieval team is that our team members and our ambulance are chosen and equipped for a specific purpose. We carry a state-of-the-art incubator and resuscitation gear and the team will always include an on-call obstetrician and/or paediatrician, depending on availability and what the job is. What we couldn't do without are the ancillary volunteer members of the team who are rostered to be here twenty-four seven to assist us.

'You are all experienced paramedics, midwives, nurses and drivers who are prepared to give up your time and use your skills to help us provide a service that has been demonstrated to save the lives of both mothers and babies. So…thank you all for being here and…welcome. I'm going to hand over to Kelly now, who's one our long-standing paramedic volunteers and has now trained to a level where she might be leading the team if our specialists are unavailable.'

Kelly could feel how every glance was on her now and she could feel her muscles tense.

She didn't want to be the centre of attention or get praised to a point where you might have people expecting you to be perfect. For them to be watching your every move, ready to pounce on any perceived faults and put you back in your place. She especially didn't want Ari to think that she had an overinflated ego. Was he staring at her as well? Kelly actually ducked her head to avoid looking up but she knew the answer to that question because she could feel that tingle in her gut again and it was as strong as some kind of electrical current.

'Kelly's going to give you a brief outline of the types of obstetric emergencies you might expect to go to and the management from a pre-hospital perspective.' Phillip was moving to sit down. 'One of our neonatal paediatricians will talk about our protocols for caring for premature infants after that, and that'll be enough for your first session. We have regular training evenings that will get you up to speed to assist with things like neonatal resuscitation and the use of incubators.'

'And we regularly finish those training evenings over at the Kensington Arms.' Kelly smiled at the group as she stood up. 'It's not all work and no fun, I promise. And

I can tell you from personal experience that you're going to meet some amazing people and learn a great deal about managing specific kinds of medical emergencies. Like our more common obstetric challenges such as major post-partum haemorrhage, a retained placenta, or an obstructed labour.'

Kelly paused and looked around a group of people who were giving her their full attention. They were putting their hands up because they wanted to make a difference to women—and their babies—who might be in serious trouble and that was something she respected.

'You know, I've given an introductory talk like this many times in the four years that I've been involved with the flying squad,' she told them. 'And I usually show you some flow charts of the protocols we follow and throw in a few boring statistics about how often these types of cases happen and what the outcomes might be but tonight I'm going to do something a bit different.

'I'm going to tell you a story about a case I went to only a week or so ago where a midwife was clued up enough to know that something serious was happening. It wasn't a callout to the flying squad but it could well have been. And it's the kind of job where you know that you've made a difference because I can tell you about how it ended for both a premature baby and a young mother—let's call her Susan—and that outcome is why we do what we do. And why I, for one, have found being a part of this team to be life-changing.'

Kelly was about to tell the story of how they'd met, wasn't she?

Ari was that "clued-up" midwife, and the compliment meant quite a lot, coming from someone whose work he respected so much. He could feel his lips were curling up on one side as, yet again, Kelly's gaze sought him out in the far corner of this group.

There was no doubt that Kelly had been pleased to see him turn up tonight. About as pleased as Peggy had been when he'd told her where he was going.

'Oh, I'm so happy. If you see that lovely Kelly again, invite her to dinner. I want to thank her for taking such good care of me last week.'

She wanted to do a lot more than that, of course. Ari had no intention of passing on an invitation that was such a blatant attempt at matchmaking but he did want a chance to talk to Kelly. He listened to her describing Vicky's signs and symptoms and refrained from joining in when she invited the group to guess what their provisional diagnosis had been.

'Premature labour?' someone suggested.

'That could certainly explain some abdominal pain but not the amount of blood loss.'

'Placenta praevia?'

'Good thought.' Kelly nodded. 'But the classic presentation is painless bleeding in the third trimester.'

'Trauma,' a young man near the front offered. 'I work as a nurse in ED and I've seen that kind of presentation. Had Susan had a car accident she thought was only minor at the time? Or a fall?'

'That wins as being the closest differential diagnosis,' Kelly told him. 'And I could add that, due to the situation we found ourselves in, we had to consider the possibility of domestic violence.'

A ripple of increased interest ran through the group. Many of these people were used to working in a controlled, clinical environment where there were security guards and plenty of colleagues if they found themselves in a dodgy situation. They were signing themselves up for frontline work in the community with all the unknowns that could bring, but they were up for it. Excited by the prospect, even. As Ari was. While there was still the worry of not being immediately available if Peggy needed him if he was on a night shift for the squad, this was exactly the kind of thing that fed his passion for the work he did. And Peggy wasn't about to back down on that deal they'd made.

Having been given the clue that what they were dealing with had very similar signs and symptoms to abdominal trauma in pregnancy, it was an easy step to discuss placental abruption and the treatment given before rushing "Susan" to hospital. Kelly finished her story with the successful outcome of the timely Caesarean and two lives that had been saved, and that was why Ari wanted to talk to her. He could give her an epilogue to that case history because he'd been up to visit Vicky earlier today when he'd been on the labour ward for a delivery.

Any chance to talk had to wait until this introductory evening was over and the group, other than those on call at the hospital, drifted down the road to the pub. And then he had to wait even longer because there were so many people keen to talk to Kelly and ask questions about her experiences with the flying squad.

'Do we really need to know everything about the settings for neonatal ventilation pressures and for the incubators? It sounded incredibly complicated.'

'The more you know, the better you can assist the specialists but you'll never be sent somewhere on your own, don't worry. If there are no doctors available for whatever reason, the job is taken over by the ambulance service—usually with a rapid response vehicle, like the one I work in, followed by transport options of either an ambulance or a helicopter.'

Even the bartender in the Kensington Arms wanted to talk to Kelly, judging by the grin on his face as he came to take her order.

'Hey…it's you again. Hope you're not still waiting for that idiot who stood you up last week.'

It was becoming familiar, that feeling of connection when Kelly's gaze caught and held his own, but this time it was a whole heap stronger. He could see amusement dancing in her eyes but, below that, he could sense what he already knew—that Kelly understood why he hadn't turned up that night and she'd not only forgiven him, she respected him for his choice.

The bartender hadn't noticed anything significant in the blink of time before Kelly smiled back.

'He's far from an idiot and it wasn't his fault. You must be used to us medical types.'

'Some of the stories I hear being told make my hair curl.' The bartender shook his head. 'And meals that get abandoned by people rushing off to an emergency? Don't know how you all do it. Now, what can I get you?'

'A glass of white wine, thanks. Small one. Ari—can I get you something?'

'Just a soda water for me. I'll have to be on my bike in a few minutes.' He took the glass from Kelly a moment later. 'I just wanted to let you know about…you know… Susan?'

'Oh?' Kelly turned back swiftly after picking up her wine. 'I've been wanting to follow up on her.'

'I just caught her packing her bag. She's about to be discharged, having made a good recovery from that emergency Caesarean.'

'And the baby? It was a boy, wasn't it?'

'It was. He's still in NICU but doing well, apparently. And…even better, there's some support in place for dealing with domestic abuse. If…um… Susan wants to take it, that is.'

'Mmm…' Kelly glanced over her shoulder but the other members of tonight's group were busy getting to know each other and weren't close enough to overhear. 'That can be tricky. People—even intelligent people—can get caught in dysfunctional relationships. It can be quite hard to escape.'

That tiny frown line between her eyes was a dead giveaway for Ari. She knew what she was talking about because she'd been there. It was as if she was offering an excuse for having been stupid enough to have been caught herself. He wanted to touch that line and smooth it away. Instead, he just made the connection that came automatically with their eye contact.

'I know how hard it can be,' he said softly. 'But thank goodness some people are brave enough to make that escape, however long it takes. Let's hope Susan is as well.'

The way Kelly's eyes widened was almost invisible but, thanks to that connection, Ari was quite sure that she'd received the message that he understood more than she might have realised. And that he applauded the effort it might have taken for her to make that escape. Not that this was the place or time to talk about it.

'How's Stacey doing?' Kelly asked hurriedly. 'And Peggy?'

'Stace is okay, I think. She finally went to an antenatal appointment. They're not sure of a due date because the best time to estimate gestational age by ultrasound is between weeks eight and eighteen. It gets less accurate after that and this baby may well be small for dates given the lifestyle Stace has been living, but she could be nearly eight months along.'

'She's still with Peggy?'

'Yes. And seems to be behaving herself. Peggy's not about to let her go back on the streets and you already know how stubborn my mum can be. Hence why I'm here tonight so that she rings the hospital tomorrow and hopefully gets a new date for surgery.'

'How's *she* doing?' That frown line had reappeared but this time it was there from a sincere concern for someone else's welfare and Ari's heart melted a little. Kelly the paramedic was a genuinely kind and caring person and the thought that anyone could have treated her badly was unacceptable.

'She's doing well,' Ari said. 'Her pain's under good control. She wanted me to pass on her thanks to you for helping her so much last week.'

'It was a real pleasure.' Kelly smiled. 'I like your mum a lot.'

'She likes you, too.'

That smile was doing something weird to Ari's brain. It seemed to be reminding him that Kelly might need someone to tell her how amazing she was. That she might need a friend. Telling him that he was quite capable of *being* that friend and ignoring any attraction that might be there. It was also undermining that resolve about what he *wasn't* going to tell her.

'She also wants you to come to dinner with us so that she can thank you herself. If that's not unethical or anything, given that she's been your patient?'

There was surprise in Kelly's eyes now but the way she caught her breath suggested that the surprise was not unpleasant.

'That depends...'

'On what?'

'On whether Peggy was simply a patient

or whether I can consider her to be a patient that's the mother of one of my colleagues from the flying squad. Or, even better, a friend's mum.'

'That's an affirmative.' Ari nodded solemnly. 'On both counts.'

It was true. He was looking forward to working on the same team she was so passionate about. He could also be a friend, if she wanted him to be—the best friend it was possible for anyone *to* be. It certainly seemed as if she liked that idea, judging by the sparkle in those amazingly blue eyes, but her tone was just as solemn as his had been.

'That's okay, then,' she said. 'I'd love to come to dinner.'

Well…this was a bit awkward.

There she was, having just knocked on Peggy's door and a text message pinged into her phone at the same moment the door was opening.

'That'll be Ari,' Peggy told her as she opened her message. 'He just rang me to say he's running a wee bit late.'

'Mmm…' Kelly was scanning the message. Ari was certain it was a false alarm but his client was anxious enough to need further reassurance so he was meeting her at the hospital.

'Come in, come in,' Peggy urged. 'And never mind about Ari. This will give us a chance to have a chat.'

The crinkles around Peggy's eyes made her smile so utterly welcoming that any awkwardness simply evaporated. Until Kelly arrived in the kitchen, that was, and found Stacey sitting at the kitchen table, glaring at her. This was the first time that Kelly had seen her properly and the teenager's face looked too thin beneath eyes that were as dark as Ari's. Her bright red hair was in long spikes on one side and shaved on the other and she had a silver ring through the bottom of her nose. Her stare was definitely unfriendly.

'What's *she* doing here?'

'I told you that one of Ari's friends was coming to dinner.' Peggy patted Stacey's shoulder as she walked past. 'Don't eat that whole bag of crisps, okay? You'll spoil your appetite for proper food.'

'She's Ari's *girlfriend*?' Stacey shook her head. 'Nah…he's never brought a girlfriend home in his life, has he?' Her huff of sound was dismissive. 'They've never lasted that long, that's why.'

'I'm just a friend,' Kelly told her. 'Ari and I are going to be working together sometimes.'

'On a *flying* squad.' Peggy made it sound like the most elite working environment possible. ''Specially for mothers and babies. Real emergencies. He'll sleep at the hospital sometimes to do a night shift. Maybe with Kelly.'

Stacey snorted. 'He'll be sleeping with Kelly?'

'*No.*' Peggy and Kelly spoke together in a mix of indignant and admonishing tones and then they looked at each other. For a beat, as they made eye contact, Kelly could see that Peggy was hoping there might be something more than friendship in her relationship with Ari. Kelly had the uncomfortable feeling that Peggy might be able to see exactly the same thing in her eyes but, if she did, it just gave the two women an understanding that closed any gap between them. And it made them both smile.

'Can I do anything to help with dinner?' Kelly asked. 'It smells wonderful but I'm not sure you should be on your feet too much.'

'It's just a roast. The oven's doing all the work. And I'm good, thanks, lovey. I've got my pills and patches sorted out so I'm not in any pain at all at the moment.' There was a mischievous twinkle in her eyes. 'Maybe I don't even need that operation.'

Kelly grinned. 'You wouldn't go back on your half of the deal, though, would you?'

Stacey held up her crisp packet to tip the last crumbs into her mouth. 'She's having the operation in a couple of weeks,' she informed Kelly. 'And I'm going to be looking after her when she gets home.'

So there...her tone suggested. *You're not needed here*...

Or maybe it was more like a warning to stay away from Ari? Kelly remembered Peggy saying that Ari had looked after Stacey when she had first arrived—a miserable baby going through drug withdrawal—and that it had been hard work, even for a baby whisperer. How many hours had he spent soothing that baby? she wondered. And how strong would the bond between them be? Did Stacey know her biological father or had Ari been the only man to help care for her as a young child, even though he would have only been a teenager himself back then? Anyway...she could understand why Stacey might feel possessive.

'It's good that you'll be here,' she told Stacey. 'I'm guessing it's quite hard to stop Peggy doing more than she probably should be doing.'

'Oh, pfff...' Peggy flapped her hand. 'Come and sit down somewhere comfy. Would you like a glass of wine? Or a cup of tea?'

'A cup of tea sounds wonderful. Oh...and I brought this for you...' Kelly handed over the box she was carrying. 'Just something for dessert. A mud cake. It can go in the freezer if you don't need it.'

'Ooh...that's your favourite, isn't it, Stace? Mud cake?'

Stacey shrugged. 'I've kind of gone off chocolate.' She pushed herself to her feet, the baggy, purple corduroy dungarees she was wearing almost hiding her bump. 'I'll be in my room,' she told Peggy.

'Don't mind her.' A few minutes later Kelly carried the tray with the teapot and cups down to the other end of the kitchen where they could sit on the couch. 'She's got a lot to cope with at the moment and she's trying hard. She's actually got a heart of gold hidden under all that angst.'

Kelly smiled. 'You must have been the

best foster mother. You see the good in everyone, don't you?'

'I try, lovey. Yes, milk and two sugars for me, thanks.' She accepted the cup with a sigh, took an appreciative sip and then caught Kelly's gaze. 'We've all got things that can hide the best of us, haven't we?'

'That's true.' Kelly knew she'd been hiding for a long time. Being here, in this house, knowing that Ari would also be here very soon, felt like she was stepping out of that hiding place and it could have scary, except that she was with an extraordinary old lady who had the ability to make you feel safe.

Like Ari did…

'Sometimes those things are a bit hard to get past,' Peggy added quietly. 'And the hardest thing of all to rebuild, after it's broken, is trust.'

Kelly swallowed hard. How could Peggy know this much about her? What had Ari said?

'I think I told you that Ari came to me when he was just a little lad?'

Kelly nodded. 'About six or seven?'

'Mmm… His mother had taken him out to a children's playground somewhere. Hyde Park, maybe? Anyway, it was supposed to be a special outing—a treat for his birthday. She must have waited until he was too busy playing to notice and she just walked away. Abandoned him. He didn't speak for weeks. Took a year to see him smile.'

Kelly's heart was breaking for that little boy. For a trust between a mother and child that should be unbreakable to have been shattered in such a brutal way. She remembered something else that Peggy had told her, too. That the first time she'd seen him smile had been when he'd been holding a baby and had managed to stop it crying. When he'd been protecting someone even more vulnerable than himself.

She had to blink hard now. That said so much about the kind of person Ari was, didn't it? It was no wonder she felt safe around him. No wonder Stacey wanted to look out for him. As she blinked away the threat of tears, Kelly found herself focusing on the blanket she was sitting on. Trying to centre herself in the present. Trying not to duck back into that hiding place because she was feeling exposed and potentially too vulnerable.

'I love this,' she told Peggy. 'It's the sort of blanket that even looks like a cuddle.'

'I've made a few of them in my time, I can

tell you. Too many. I give them away now, although I've started a new one for Stacey so she can wrap herself up when she's feeding the baby in the night. If she decides to keep it, that is.' Peggy closed her eyes for a heartbeat, as if she was in pain, but she was smiling brightly again as soon she opened her eyes. 'I meant the baby,' she whispered. 'It's not hard to keep a blanket, is it?'

Kelly smiled back, taking the hint that the atmosphere needed lightening. 'I've always wanted to learn to knit,' she admitted. 'I'd love to make something like this.'

'It's the perfect way to learn, making granny squares. Do you know they're actually called Peggy squares, too? After the little girl who started making them in the Depression. And, there's no time like the present, I always say.' Peggy put down her tea cup and reached into a cavernous bag beside her end of the couch. 'I've got some needles and wool right here. Look, I'll cast on for you and you'll be knitting by the time dinner's ready.'

It always felt like home letting himself in through that red front door but it was even more of a comfort this evening.

Maybe it was because Ari was starving, having missed lunch and then been caught late at the hospital when he was more than ready for his dinner. The enticing smell of a roasting chicken was the first thing he was aware of as he stepped back into his childhood home. The second thing, almost simultaneously noticed, was a peal of laughter. A laugh he'd never heard before but he knew instantly that it was Kelly who was laughing and knowing that she was enjoying herself even if the evening hadn't started off quite as planned gave Ari a ripple of pleasure. Or maybe it was the sound of that laughter that was giving him that sensation. And maybe that ripple wasn't simply pleasure because it came along with a knot in his gut that felt very different from something as shallow as mere enjoyment. But it didn't feel quite like attraction either. It actually felt like a knot. Complicated and hard to unravel.

He passed Stacey's room on his way to the kitchen and paused when he saw her lying on her bed through the open door.

'Not hungry, Stace?'

'Nah…'

'You want to come and keep us company, anyway?'

'What, you and your *girlfriend*? No, thanks.'

Ari took a step further into her room. 'She's not my girlfriend.'

That knot tightened another notch so that it was almost painful and, at the same time, his stomach rumbled. Perhaps it wasn't being caused by anything emotional at all and it was nothing more than hunger, which could be easily fixed.

'She's just a friend.' He added, as further reassurance to a young girl who seemed to be looking for reasons why she wasn't wanted, 'As if I've got time for a girlfriend when I've got you and Mum to look after at the moment.'

There was a beat of silence broken by the sound of a frustrated groan from the direction of the kitchen, followed by a murmur from Peggy and then more laughter.

'She's trying to learn how to knit,' Stacey told Ari. 'And you know what?'

'What?'

'She sucks.'

'Hey…' Ari put on a stern face. 'We all suck when we try something for the first time. What counts is sucking that up so that you can get to be good at it.' He turned away. 'You might not be hungry but, man, I could eat a horse and whatever Mum's cooking smells amazing.'

He could hear the sound of Stacey's boots hitting the floor behind him as he left the room.

'Maybe I am a bit hungry, after all,' she said.

CHAPTER FIVE

'ARE YOU SURE you've got time for this?'

'Absolutely.' Kelly opened the back doors of the ambulance that was parked in a reserved slot at the edge of the bay outside Kensington's emergency department. 'Unless there's a call for the flying squad, in which case I'll be in exactly the right place, won't I? Jump in,' she invited. 'If you're sure you've got the time?'

'I'm back early from house calls.' Ari climbed into the ambulance. 'I've got at least half an hour before my outpatient clinic starts. Unless I get a call myself, of course. Babies have a mind of their own sometimes.'

'Don't they just? Pull those doors shut so we can keep the rain out.' Kelly could feel goosebumps where the tunic of her scrub suit left her arms bare. Was it just the chilly weather or did it have something to do with being shut in a confined space with Ari Lawson? It certainly seemed to accentuate his size and that sheer masculinity.

Kelly cleared her throat, hurriedly searching for something else to focus on. 'So…here we are. This is our squad truck. It's set up a bit differently from a normal ambulance. We've got the two incubators, in case we dealing with twins, and the seating for the two crew members. If we're transporting the mother as well, she sits up front with the driver or, if it's an obstetric emergency we're usually backing up a normal ambulance crew so they've got the stretcher. Our third crew sits up front, too, if we've got someone on an orientation shift. Has someone contacted you or have you put your name down for one yet?'

'Not yet. Peggy's waitlisted in case there's a gap due to a cancelation so she might not get much notice for her surgery. Could be any day. I'll put my name down as soon as we know what's happening.' Ari was looking around at all the monitoring equipment and the built-in storage for a wealth of supplies. 'You look set up to deal with major interventions here.'

'We have two main kinds of scenarios. One is to cut out-of-hospital time for a sick baby as much as possible so we do low-level interventions like a peripheral IV, nasogastric tube, oxygen and then we hit the road. What we like to call a "swoop and scoop" job.'

Ari was listening intently, his gaze fixed on Kelly. It was easier to hold that eye contact when she was talking about something professional like this but it didn't stop that frisson of something that was certainly not at all professional which eye contact with this man always seemed to generate.

'And the other main scenario? Is that a "stay and play", like we had with Vicky?'

The reminder of how they'd met and her first impressions of Ari made Kelly realise how much their friendship had developed since then. There was a familiarity about his company now and after that visit to his home and getting a glimpse into what was important in his life, it seemed like Kelly was further along a path to them becoming so much closer and that was tantalising. Scary but compelling at the same time. Even listening to his voice was delicious because it was as deep and dark as his eyes and it had just a hint of a gravelly edge to it. Everything about Ari was classically masculine. Apart from his job, that was. And the way he wore his hair. Maybe that was all part of the attraction—the things that made him stand out as being so different…

'Pretty much.' Amazing how thoughts—and feelings—could flash by so fast nobody else would ever guess what you might be thinking. Ari hadn't even noticed any hesitation in Kelly's response. 'That's where we stabilise the baby as much as possible before leaving the referring hospital or scene and that might involve intubation, arterial or central venous cannulation or sometimes it might be something like artificial surfactant administration for extreme respiratory failure or a chest drain to deal with a pneumothorax. Depends what expertise we have on board. They're not cut-and-dried boundaries either. Often it ends up being a combination, although it's preferable not to have to stop to initiate anything major, like intubation or CPR.'

'How do you manage CPR on a baby in an incubator?'

'We get it out. Look, there's a great feature on this travel incubator with a slide-out mattress.' Kelly demonstrated how easy it was to get the kind of access they would need to start CPR. 'Quick as...'

'That's very cool.'

Ari moved to help Kelly slide the mattress back into place and, as his hand brushed hers, she felt her breath catch. Skin contact was even more charged than eye contact and had far more effect than the sound of his voice. Was Ari aware of the same sensation—as if one's skin had suddenly become a whole lot more sensitive? If he was, he was hiding it well. His attention was on the features of this state-of-the-art transport incubator.

'So...those tubing ports are to allow for monitoring leads for the ECG, continuous blood pressure and pulse oximetry without heat or humidity loss,' Kelly told him. 'Did I hear that you've got a qualification in neonatal resuscitation? The team were really impressed with the postgraduate study you've clocked up.'

Ari nodded. 'That was an amazing course. I'd done the basics, of course, but there was so much to learn about the physiology, especially with resuscitating premature babies. It's a delicate balance, isn't it? The first priority is to get lungs inflated but you have to be so gentle with how much pressure you use and so careful about oxygen administration.'

'Mmm...' Kelly's gaze was on Ari's hands as he spoke. She'd seen him working so she knew how capable and gentle he was with his touch. She could imagine him working on tiny babies that he could probably cup in the palm of his hand, and this time it wasn't so much of a tingle of attraction that she was aware of. More like a squeeze of something rather more poignant. Like seeing a fireman holding a tiny kitten could spark, or a burly guy stopping to help an old lady across a road. The thought of that little old lady was enough to distract her completely from what was supposed to be a purely professional meeting to show Ari the way the flying squad's ambulance was set up.

'How's Peggy?' she found herself asking. 'I was a bit worried the other night. She didn't eat much of that lovely dinner she'd cooked, did she? Is she worried about the surgery?'

'Only because she won't be around to keep an eye on Stacey. She's worried she might go back to the group she was living with. There's a boy involved, by the sound of things.'

'The father of the baby?'

Ari shrugged. 'Don't know. Don't think so but, if it is, she's not saying. I suspect Peggy's the only person she really trusts but I get that. Hope you weren't offended by her attitude.'

Kelly shook her head and then smiled. 'She doesn't like me much, does she?'

'She doesn't like anyone or any*thing* much right now. Including herself. I'm not too sure of the best way to handle any of this—I've been away from home for too long. I haven't even seen Stace since she was about fourteen.'

'She's lucky to have Peggy in her corner.'

'Anyone who gets Peggy in their corner is lucky,' Ari agreed.

His smile was enough to give Kelly's heart another huge squeeze. 'I've only just met her,' she said quietly, 'but I feel lucky that she's touched my life as well. She's an extraordinary woman, isn't she? Her house…that dinner we had…it felt like, I don't know…a real family.'

Ari's smile widened. 'Complete with the angsty teenager.'

'I was an only child,' Kelly told him, 'and my parents were very absorbed by their academic careers. I never really got that feeling of family and I've always felt like there was something missing from my life.'

'You'll find it,' Ari told her quietly. 'You can create your own one day.'

Kelly shrugged. 'Maybe.' She hadn't found anything like that so far, though. Quite the opposite.

'Biology creates relatives,' Ari added. 'It's love that creates family and it's never too late to find that.'

'So friends can be family?' Kelly caught his gaze again, a tiny part of her brain almost counting down to when that frisson would arrive.

'Absolutely.' The gaze from those dark eyes softened and it felt like a comforting touch.

And…there it was. Only this time it was strong enough to feel painful. This wasn't simply attraction, it was desire. Strong enough for the scary element to be noticeably ramped up, given the disaster that had come from the last time she'd given in to feelings like this. Her time with Darryn had been so destructive that she'd run from any hint of interest from—or in—another man.

But this felt safer.

Perhaps it was because of Stacey's dismissive comment the other night about how girlfriends never lasted long enough to be invited home. Or Peggy's gentle warning about how hard it was for Ari to trust women. Kelly might be attracted but there was no chance at all that she was going to make the first move. She knew what it was like to find it hard to trust. How easy it was to get scared into running back to a safe place—the way she'd been running for years.

And, if Ari did that, she wouldn't be able to spend time with him. Even if they could only ever be just friends, it was something she definitely didn't want to risk losing.

'Let me know when Peggy's surgery is scheduled, won't you? I'll be there as soon as she's up for visitors.' Her smile felt slightly wobbly. 'I want to show her the squares I've knitted. It's taken nearly a whole ball of wool but I'm getting better at it. I might even go and buy some more wool.'

'I remember going to charity shops with Peggy when I was a kid. There's usually a basket of odd balls of wool in a corner somewhere. She'd let me choose all the brightest colours. She made me a blanket when I left home and I've still got it.'

'Bring one of those blankets in, when she's admitted,' Kelly suggested. 'If I was in a hospital bed, it would make me feel better.'

'That's a great idea.' But Ari's face looked sombre. Thoughtful. 'You're a nice person, Kelly. Special...'

Kelly swallowed hard. Look away, she told herself. Don't make this something it isn't. But it was Ari who looked away first. Abruptly.

'Is that the time? I'm going to have to run.'

To the maternity wing's outpatient department? Or to his safe place?

Not that it mattered. Kelly might not be running from the awareness of how attracted she was to Ari but she still needed those boundaries as much as he did. And perhaps that was where the real feeling of safety was coming from—knowing that you could step behind that invisible line and the safety it provided was going to be not only understood but respected.

The woman in the charity shop who took Kelly's money for the balls of wool a day or two later looked almost as old as Peggy. She cast an admiring glance at Kelly's uniform.

'You work on the ambulance, don't you?'

'I do. I've got a few minutes spare at the moment, though, because I'm on my lunch break—I'm not really skiving off to go shopping.'

'I'm sure you're not.'

The balls of wool were being counted as they got put into a paper bag. Kelly had bought a few more than she probably needed but she wanted to replace the one that Peggy had kindly given her, along with that first pair of knitting needles. She wasn't that far from the old house, in fact, so she might have time to pop in for a quick visit.

'Wonderful job you folk do,' the woman continued. 'I needed an ambulance once myself, you know…when I took a funny turn at the supermarket. I— *Oh…*'

They were both startled by the loud thump and rattle of someone hitting the plate-glass window of the charity shop behind the woman who was in charge of the till. For a moment, as she saw the look of terror on the elderly woman's face, Kelly was worried that she might have to deal with another "funny turn", but her attention swiftly shifted to what was happening on the other side of the window. An unkempt and angry young man had shoved a girl so that her back had slammed into the window. He still had his hands on her shoulders and he looked as though he was about to start shaking her. The glass was fortunately thick enough not to shatter under the impact, but it wasn't thick enough to totally mute the swearing and insults being thrown at the girl.

'Why can't you just do what I tell you to do, you stupid, ugly bitch? Too stupid to live, that's your problem. Can't think what I ever saw in you...'

'Oh, my...' The charity shop volunteer had her hand to her chest. 'Young people these days...it must be drugs or something, surely? Should I call the police, do you think?'

Kelly could only see the girl's back but she'd known instantly exactly who it was. Nobody else could have that half-spiky, half-shaved scarlet hair teamed with a pair of purple dungarees.

Kelly shook her head. 'I'll see if I can deal with it. If I can't then I'll call the police on my radio. They might get here quicker that way. You stay in here.'

It was a very good thing she was in her uniform, Kelly decided as she stormed out of the shop. Not only did she have that radio clipped to her belt so she could call for urgent assistance if needed, just the sight of someone in uniform was enough to startle and then intimidate the man who was threatening Stacey. He gave her another shove against the window, hard enough to make the glass rattle again, and then spat on the footpath as he took off, pushing through the knot of people who had stopped to see what was going on.

Stacey looked frozen for a moment as she took in the fact that her attacker had gone, that she was being stared at by a small crowd of people and that Kelly was standing beside her, looking official in her uniform.

'*What*?' she shouted at the onlookers. 'Take a picture, why don't you?'

Kelly could sense how scared the teenager was under her aggressive bravado. 'Come with me.' She put a hand on Stacey's arm. 'My car's just over there. I'll take you home.'

Stacey shook her arm free. 'I don't want to go home.'

'You want to talk to the police instead? The lady in the charity shop might have rung them already.'

That lady was coming towards them, in fact. 'Here,' she said, handing Kelly a paper bag. 'Don't forget this.' She stared at Stacey.

'Are you all right?' she asked. 'Who was that lout and why was he hitting you?'

'He wasn't hitting me,' Stacey muttered. 'And it's none of your beeswax, anyway, so shut up...'

'Well, I never...' The older woman tutted at the rude tone. 'Keep it away from my shop in future. Go and break someone else's window. I know what you look like, young lady, and I can give your description to the police.'

'This way...' This time, Kelly's hand didn't allow her hand to get shaken off. 'In the car. Now—before you get yourself into any more trouble. And put your safety belt on. I'm taking you home.'

She started the vehicle and pulled into the traffic. 'So...who was that? A friend of yours? Boyfriend?' If he was the boy Ari had heard about, he looked like trouble.

Stacey turned to stare out of the side window, clearly having no intention of responding. All Kelly could catch a glimpse of was the back of her head and her hunched shoulders. Taking a slow breath in, Kelly tried to channel some of Peggy's patience. What actually came into her head, though, was an image of a young Ari holding a tiny, miserable baby who was suffering from the effects of the drugs her mother had been taking while she was pregnant. She could imagine those strong arms sheltering the infant. She could even imagine how it would feel to be within that hold and, suddenly, that was more than enough to give her the patience and strength not to allow herself to be irritated enough to step back from this troubled girl. To try and step closer, even, and find a connection that might help.

'Maybe it isn't any of my business,' she said quietly. 'But I've been there, Stacey. That boy might not have been hitting you hard enough to leave a mark but even getting yelled at and being called names is still abuse. You don't deserve that. Don't let him put you down.'

She'd been watching the road as she spoke but, from the corner of her eye, she could see Stacey's head turning. She could feel the disbelieving stare.

'*You've* been there? What's that supposed to mean?'

'I was in an abusive relationship. For a lot longer than I should have been.'

'Is that what you told Ari? To make him like you so much?'

The words slipped past but Kelly knew

she'd be thinking about that later. Not about the idea she might try and use her story to garner sympathy, though. What really mattered from those words was what "so much" might mean and why Stacey might have got that impression.

'Actually, you're the first person I've ever told,' Kelly said. 'It's not something a lot of people can understand—unless they've experienced it themselves.' She was silent for a moment. 'I'm sorry you're being treated like that. You deserve better.'

'What would you know? You don't even know me.' Stacey had wrapped her arms around herself. 'I'm nothing like you. My boyfriend's right—I'm rubbish. Just a nobody.' The words were flooding out now. 'Look at me. I'm only seventeen and I'm pregnant and I don't even know who the father is. I don't know who *my* father is and my mum did a runner years ago.' She was sobbing now. 'I've never had a family...'

Kelly pulled the SUV to the side of the road and sent up a silent plea that her radio wasn't about to crackle into life and demand that she take off somewhere else.

She reached for the box of tissues in the central console and handed Stacey a handful.

'That's not true,' she said. 'You've got two of the most amazing people that I've ever met in your life. Peggy's been caring about you since you were born. So has Ari. I've only spent one evening in your house and it felt like a family to me. It's something special and I think you know that.'

Stacey didn't bother with the tissues, ignoring the tears streaming from her eyes and her running nose. 'Peggy's going to die soon and Ari'll disappear back to his flash job in Scotland and they'll take my baby away to give it to someone who can look after it properly and then what?' Her voice rose. 'I'll have nothing. No one...'

Patience could be pushed just a bit too far. Kelly could feel anger building at the way Peggy and Ari's love for this teenager was being dismissed. She could also feel immense sadness that Peggy might be close to the end of her life and having to deal with an attitude that was so completely undeserved.

'I know you're only seventeen,' she said, keeping her tone level. 'And I know life hasn't been easy for you but...here's a newsflash, Stacey. It's not always all about *you*.'

Stacey's hiccup was a shocked sound but she had stopped crying.

'You've got good people in your corner—amazing people—and you've still got your whole life in front of you,' Kelly continued. 'There's no reason you can't turn things around and become whatever you want to be but right now it's Peggy who needs to be cared for. She's given you so much and all you can think about is how you're going to be affected when she's gone. Can't you see how selfish that is? You know what she's doing? The present she's making for you?'

Stacey's gaze was downcast, her chin tucked into her chest, but she shook her head.

'She's knitting peggy squares to make a special blanket. She wants you to be warm if you're up in the night feeding your baby. The way she probably got up in the night countless times to feed *you*.' Kelly was close to tears herself now as she reached for the paper bag that she'd tucked in beside the tissues and pulled out a ball of wool. 'Here.' She shoved it into Stacey's hands. 'Take this and give it to Peggy from me. She might need it to finish that blanket.' She turned away and put her hands on the steering wheel. 'You can walk home from here. It's not far.'

She had to clear her throat as a beep announced an incoming radio message.

'Rover One, are you receiving?'

'Rover One,' she replied. 'Receiving you loud and clear.'

'Code Red call. Stand by for details.'

'Standing by...'

Stacey had already unclipped her safety belt. Kelly dismissed her with a nod as the teenager opened the door and climbed out of her vehicle. She had turned on her beacons by the time the door was slammed shut and was ready to program the address into her satnav before she pulled out onto the road again and took off, flicking her siren into life.

There was a child choking only half a mile away. Kelly didn't look back.

Ari Lawson glanced up at the clock on the wall of the waiting room and then closed his eyes for a moment. How could time be moving this slowly? Peggy had only been in Theatre for a little over an hour but it felt like he'd been waiting for a lot longer.

'You're still here... I thought I might be too late.'

His eyes flew open and something with the force of a fist slammed into his gut. In a good way, that was. Seeing Kelly was the best surprise he could have had. A reprieve from being alone in this vigil with his memories and fears for what the near future might hold. 'Too late for what?'

'To keep you company. I had a feeling you'd be pacing around in here.' Kelly's gaze raked the otherwise empty room. 'Stacey didn't come in?'

'She said she hates hospitals. And she's got stuff she wanted to do. I said I'd ring as soon as Peggy's out of Theatre.'

'How long since she went in?' Kelly perched on the chair beside Ari.

'Over an hour ago.'

'Did they tell you how long it might take?'

'A while. They couldn't be precise. They're doing a full hysterectomy and probably need to remove a section of bowel as well so it could be quite a while. Don't feel you have to stay.'

He wanted her to stay, though, didn't he? So much so it felt more like a need than a want.

'I don't have any other place to be…' Ari might be getting used to that lovely smile of Kelly's but seeing it was never going to get old. 'And look…' Kelly opened her shoulder bag to show him what was inside. 'I've got my knitting. I can get another peggy square done. Maybe two. I'm getting faster now.'

Ari smiled. 'Peggy will be proud of you. She'll be very touched when I tell her that you came to wait, too. She already thinks that you're some kind of angel.'

Kelly ducked her head, clearly embarrassed. Was she remembering that first time she met his foster mother—when she'd said that it was about time Ari met a nice girl like her? Had she also realised that that dinner invitation had been an attempt at matchmaking on Peggy's part?

If so, it didn't seem to be standing in the way of them becoming friends. Okay, there was that undercurrent of attraction that he was pretty sure was mutual, but he also knew that Kelly wasn't going to act on it and neither was he. It was just there. Something they could ignore because, for whatever reason, neither of them wanted anything more in their lives. And that was fine by Ari because it meant that they could be real friends with no expectations of it turning into anything more than that. No pressure. No strings. It was more than fine, really. More like perfect.

Conversation was easy because they had the same interests, thanks to their work. Ari told Kelly that someone from the O&G department had contacted him to see if he was available for an observer shift with the flying squad on the coming Sunday.

'Really? I'm doing a day shift that day. It would be cool if you had your first shift with me but… Peggy will still be in hospital, won't she?'

'Which is exactly why it might be a good time to do it. If it's not busy, I can visit. It's a day shift so I wouldn't be leaving Stace alone at night. And, if it is busy, I'd have lots to tell Peggy about when I visit on Monday.'

'She'd love that. She really loved her work as a midwife, didn't she?'

'She adored babies. It's sad she didn't get to have any of her own but…if she had, I guess there'd be dozens of kids who didn't get to share that love. Kids like Stacey.'

Kelly's fingers slowed as she carefully wound her wool around the needle. 'And like you. Peggy told me a little bit about how you came to be with her. How long it took you to feel safe. She's the one who's the angel. How hard would it be to be that patient and just keep loving someone until they were ready to love you back?'

Ari had to swallow hard. He couldn't

remember those early years that well but, yeah…the love was there—on both sides—and it was so powerful it made the fear of loss hit hard. Another glance at the clock. Nearly two hours now. What was happening in that operating theatre? Was it going well? Well enough to mean that Peggy might be in his life for a bit longer?

He needed to think about something else because if he let his brain latch onto the other possible scenarios, it could undermine the strength he was going to need to support Peggy. And Stacey.

'Stacey's doing some housework. Cleaning the oven today, would you believe?'

'Wow.' Kelly's glance was astonished. 'No, I'm not sure I do believe that.'

'She wants to get out in the garden if it ever stops raining, too. Said she's going to go to the charity shop and see if they've got some gardening tools.' He was watching Kelly's fingers as she looped more wool and did complicated things with the knitting needles. 'She told me she saw *you* there the other day.'

'Mmm.' Kelly didn't look up. 'I was following that good advice you gave me. Remember? About it being a good place to go and get some cheap wool? Did…um…did she say anything else?'

'Not really.' But that was when he'd noticed a change in Stacey's attitude, though. 'Why? Did you say something to her?'

'Kind of…' Kelly sounded cautious. 'She was with a boy who looked like he had some issues. I told her that it wasn't just physical stuff that was abuse and that she should know that she deserves better than that. I might have also said that she was being pretty selfish thinking only about herself instead of Peggy.'

'Well, seems like you got through to her more than I've been able to, so thanks for that. I'm beginning to think I can trust her to do a good job of looking after Peggy when she gets home and that'll make life easier for all of us.'

'Let me know if I can help. I'd really like to…'

The knitting was forgotten as Kelly looked up and caught his gaze. They were that dark shade of blue that made Ari think again that it was emotion that had deepened their colour. Sincerity. An ability to care about others on a level that was a rare quality. Peggy had it. Maybe Stacey had been impressed by it. It was something that touched Ari on a very deep level because it tapped into the very foundations of what had changed his own life so profoundly.

He held Kelly's gaze. 'I will. Peggy would love that. I reckon Stacey would be happy to see you again, too.'

'Really?'

'Really.' Ari could feel his lips curving gently. 'And what you told her? It goes both ways, you know.'

'How d'you mean?'

'You said that Stacey deserved something better than being abused.' His smile was fading but he held that eye contact. 'So do you.'

Oh…help…

Ari wanted to put his arms around Kelly but not simply to give her a friendly hug to convey understanding, or encouragement to tell him her story if she was ready. No…at this moment, he couldn't take his eyes off her face. Her eyes. Her lips…

He wanted to hold her all right.

But what he wanted to do even more was to kiss her. To put his lips against hers and see if there was a reason that this magnetic pull was so overwhelmingly powerful. That desire was just hanging there in the air between them in a silence that was increasingly significant. A balancing act that could have gone either way. All it needed was a tiny push and if that had come from Kelly, he would have been kissing her senseless in a heartbeat. Luckily the push came from an unexpected direction and it was exactly what Ari needed to get complete control.

'Mr Lawson?' The nurse in the doorway of the waiting area was smiling. 'Your mum's out of Theatre now. Would you like to come and see her in Recovery?'

CHAPTER SIX

IT WAS STILL raining on the following Sunday.

Peggy was sitting up in her corner bed by the window but she wasn't looking at the dismal weather outside, like Ari was. She had several brightly coloured knitted squares in front of her and she was beaming at Kelly.

'Look at that. You'll have enough to make a blanket in no time. I'll have to teach you how to crochet around the edges and join them together.'

'I'd like that.' Kelly smiled back. 'You look like you're feeling better today.'

'I'm ready to go home. Three days of lying around like this is more than enough.'

'Don't think so.' Ari turned back from the window. 'You've had major surgery. You need to stay in here and rest for as long as they let you.'

'What's Stacey doing today? I do wish she'd come in and visit me.'

'I think she was planning to tidy up a bit today.'

Ari's glance shifted to where Kelly was sitting on the other side of Peggy's bed and she couldn't miss the twinkle of an understanding that was just between them. It seemed that Stacey's new attitude was continuing and Ari thought that Kelly had influenced the positive change.

'I tried to persuade her to come and visit,' he told Peggy. 'But she's got a real phobia about hospitals.'

'I know…' Peggy sighed. 'She needs to get over that before she has that baby. I don't want her having a home birth. I'd never forgive myself if something went wrong. Has she even been back to those antenatal classes?'

'I'm not sure,' Ari admitted. 'She said she went but who knows?'

'I'll make sure she goes when I get back home.'

'You won't be doing anything to stress you out. I'll be making sure of that.'

Peggy shifted her gaze to Kelly. 'So, how's

my boy doing? Have you been anywhere exciting yet?'

'No. Nowhere at all today. It's the quietest shift I've ever had with the flying squad. A bit boring, to be honest.'

Except that wasn't really true, was it? Being in Ari's company could never be considered boring, even if there was absolutely nothing to do. Especially not after what Kelly had imagined had happened just a few days ago in that waiting room. When it had felt like he'd been about to kiss her. She had *wanted* him to kiss her—so badly that the disappointment of that interruption had been crushing at the time, although when she'd relived that moment later, more than once, she'd realised that it was a good thing it hadn't happened. She wasn't ready for anything more than a friendship. It was confusing to even imagine it. Scary. It was just as well there'd been no hint of anything like that today.

'There is a possibility that a woman who's pregnant with triplets and was admitted for bed rest last week might be having a Caesarean later this afternoon,' she told Peggy. 'If we're still here we might be allowed to be in Theatre to observe.'

'I'm not bored at all,' Ari protested. 'I'm

reading up on all the protocols for handling preemie babies. We've got special plastic bags to put them in so they don't get cold. What did you do, back in the day, Ma?'

'We certainly didn't have all the bells and whistles you've got these days so we just did what we could and hoped for the best. I do remember things changing after President Kennedy's baby died. Suddenly there was more money and research being done.'

'JFK? I didn't know he lost a baby.'

'Oh…poor Jackie Kennedy had a terrible time of it. She had a miscarriage and then a stillbirth before she had the two babies that survived. And then there was the preemie baby who only lived a couple of days because of respiratory distress. We were all talking about it at work. I think I remember that they put that poor wee baby into one of those chambers for people who have diving accidents.'

'A hyperbaric chamber?'

'That's the one.' Peggy shifted a little and winced but ignored any pain she was having. 'It was to try and force oxygen into his lungs.'

Again, Ari and Kelly shared a glance. They would be talking about that soon, she thought. About how barbaric the treatment seemed now that they knew the damage that too much oxygen could do and about the improvements in managing the risks that came with undeveloped lungs—like giving the mother steroids if there was time before the birth or giving the babies artificial surfactant as protection. But that discussion was going to have to wait. Kelly's pager sounded at the same moment she caught Ari's gaze.

'Ooh…what's happening?' Peggy tried to sit up as Kelly was reading her pager and this time the pain made her gasp.

'Just rest,' Ari told her. 'And tell your nurse that you're hurting. You're allowed as much pain relief as you need, you know.' He turned back to Kelly. 'Do we need to go?'

Her nod was crisp. 'Looks like we're needed. Finally…'

'I'll be back later,' Ari told Peggy. 'If you've rested enough, I'll tell you all about it.'

'It sounds complicated,' Kelly told him as they sped down a staircase and headed for the emergency department and their vehicle. 'Premature labour but the ambulance crew can't get to her yet—there's a flooded stream that's made part of a bridge collapse. Even worse, she's trapped in her vehicle. The fire service is on its way but they're under pressure due to this weather. We might well be on scene before them.'

The call out got even more complicated when they arrived in ED to be told that they had a driver—Bruce—but there were no obstetricians or neonatal paediatricians that were available to go with them. Apparently, the Caesarean for the woman carrying triplets had just become an emergency and all staff were needed in Theatre.

'What do we do?' Ari asked.

'We'll still go,' Kelly said. She opened a cupboard to hand him a heavy-duty raincoat with fluorescent stripes. 'We've got equipment that's not available otherwise and I'm qualified to use it.' She bit her lip. 'I just prefer to be assisting the real experts.'

'You know what?' Ari raised his voice against the sound of the heavy rain as he followed Kelly outside.

'What?'

'I've seen you in action and I know how amazing you are. You can handle anything.'

'I don't know about that.' Kelly automatically dismissed the compliment, although a part of her brain—or perhaps it was actually a part of her heart—registered and liked the fact that Ari thought she was amazing, even if it wasn't true. 'Let's hope we can both handle anything. You're being thrown in at the deep end, that's for sure. Your first callout and you certainly won't be just an observer.'

This was way more exciting than Ari had expected. Not only was it the first time he'd been in an ambulance under lights and sirens but they were heading into a situation that could be life-threatening for both a mother and baby. That they had the weather against them as well added another degree of difficulty and the fact that he was with Kelly, who'd been dispatched as the lead medic for this advanced back-up in an emergency, made it all the more thrilling.

He'd meant what he'd said about her being able to handle anything but he could sense that she was nervous and he was going to give her whatever assistance he could. And maybe it was just a side effect of so much adrenaline in his system but Ari had the feeling that the two of them could make a perfect team. That, together, they could both achieve way more than if either of them was working alone.

Twenty minutes later, when they turned down a side road, having cleared one of London's outer suburbs and arrived on the scene of this emergency, it was Ari's turn to feel a beat of nervousness. He'd never had to deal with anything like this in his life. A police car was blocking the road that led to a narrow bridge. An ambulance was parked just beyond that but its crew was simply standing beside their vehicle. The beacons of both emergency vehicles flashed brightly against the driving rain and were reflected in the tumbling water of the swollen stream.

The far bank had collapsed, presumably due to the pressure of water combined with already saturated ground, and a car had come off the road and was tilted down at the bottom of the bank and seemed to be wedged on the driver's side amongst low-lying branches of a weeping willow. The water was flowing swiftly around the front tyres of the car and Ari could see a police officer on the bridge.

'Stay here, Bruce,' Kelly instructed their driver. 'Keep the engine running and the heat up as high as you can. We'll go and find out what's happening here.' She caught Ari's gaze as she handed him a heavy-duty torch. 'Ready?'

Ari took the torch, having slipped his arms into the straps of the portable kit. 'Ready,' he confirmed.

And he was. Any nervousness evaporated at that instant, replaced by adrenaline and backed up by catching some of that determination he could see in Kelly's eyes.

It was noisier than Ari might have expected. The rain and wind and the rushing water of the stream was a background to the sound of radios crackling, voices shouting, the faint sound of a siren in the distance, which could be more emergency vehicles coming their way and…more disturbingly, a cry that sounded like that of a terrified woman. He was right beside Kelly as they went past the police car blocking the road and got to the ambulance.

'We've been told not to go any further yet.' One of the young paramedics looked frustrated. 'The fire service is on its way but the car needs to be secured. There's a danger it'll get washed out from where it is and could roll. That stream is getting deeper in the middle. Plus, they don't know how stable the rest of the bridge is and they don't want any more weight on it.'

'But you know there's a pregnant woman in the car? In labour?'

'We're going on what's been relayed by the police officer on the bridge. Her name's Zoe and she's thirty-six weeks along. Her contractions had started before she went off the bridge. Her foot's caught under the pedals or something and she can't get out, even though the doors on the other side are open.'

'How far away are the firefighters?'

'Don't know. Feels like we've been waiting for ever.'

Ari turned to catch Kelly's gaze. They'd only been on scene for a matter of minutes but it already felt like far too long a delay to being with their patient. He raised his eyebrows in a silent question that Kelly seemed to understand instantly and she apparently agreed with his summing up of the situation so far—that they weren't necessarily going to comply with orders from the police officers on site if they were not in the best interests of their patient. He and Kelly could weigh up the risks and make their own decisions about what could or could not be done for the woman trapped in her car.

'Keep your truck as warm as possible,'

Kelly told the paramedics. 'If we can get her out, we might need to deliver a baby in there.'

And if they couldn't get her out, what then? Would they be delivering a baby in a car under threat of either being washed away or submerged in flood waters? This was dangerous but it didn't feel like Ari had a choice. That Kelly was brave enough to be prepared to go with him made him feel proud to be with her. Proud *of her*. He lengthened his stride. There wasn't a minute to lose and the police officer on the bridge must have sensed that neither he nor Kelly were going to be put off getting to the accident victim.

'Be careful,' was all he said. 'That ground's unstable and so is the car. The bridge is still falling apart as well. The firefighters have had to go around the long way to get to this side of the bridge. If you wait another ten minutes, they could be able to secure the vehicle.'

'*Help*…' The cry came from the car beneath them. 'Please…someone, *help*…'

'Can't wait, mate,' Ari told the police officer. 'I think we're needed.' But he turned back to Kelly before stepping onto the rubble between the bridge and the bank. The urge to protect her from danger was too difficult to suppress completely. 'Maybe you should stay up here?'

Kelly simply shook her head, dismissing the suggestion.

Ari was tall enough to reach a tree branch to use as an anchor as he started to pick his way down the slippery mud on the bank. He held his other arm out as a safety barrier for Kelly and it was needed almost immediately as she began a slide that only stopped as she grabbed hold of his arm.

'Hold on tight,' he told her. 'I've got this.'

It got easier as they got further down because the branches were lower. They could see the open, crumpled doors of the passenger side of the car. They could also see the pale face of the terrified driver.

'Oh, thank God…you're here. Please… I can't get out and I'm having… *Ahh…*' She screwed her eyes shut as she cried out in pain.

Ari was almost at the side of the car.

'You want to be in the front or the back?' he asked Kelly.

He expected her to want to get in the front passenger side to be able to get to the woman more easily. She was in charge here after all and he was only supposed to be an observer. But Kelly said she would get into the back seat.

'You've got way more experience than me in assessing how close someone is to giving birth. Put the kit in the back seat as well. There'll be more room for me to open it there.'

'Okay.' Part of Ari still wasn't happy with the idea of Kelly getting into the car at all but he couldn't ask her to stand back and watch and he wasn't about to suggest that she stay somewhere safe because he admired her courage and he wanted to work with her. He *needed* that extra dimension that the two of them could make as a team. But he touched her arm.

'Don't get in until after me, okay? If there's any danger that changing the balance is going to push the car into the current, it's best if it's only one of us in there.'

It was already darker than normal for this time of day due to the weather conditions. Now they were beneath a veil of leafy branches and the interior of the car made it feel like night-time. Ari flicked on his torch.

'Hey…' He eased himself carefully onto the front passenger seat of the car, praying that it wouldn't be enough of a change to give the current the power to do more damage. 'It's Zoe, right? I'm Ari. I'm a midwife.'

The pain from Zoe's contraction was clearly easing and her expression changed from pain to something more like horror. It wasn't because of his gender, however—simply his specialty. 'A midwife? Oh…no… there's no way I'm having a baby in here. I can't… Oh… *God*…'

'We're here to look after you,' Ari told her. 'You and the baby.' The car wasn't showing any sign that it was going to start moving so he gave Kelly a nod. 'That's Kelly getting into the back seat now,' he told Zoe. 'She's an awesome paramedic and she's part of the obstetric flying squad so you're in good hands, okay?'

But Zoe had a hand covering her eyes. 'I just want to get out,' she sobbed. 'I want to go home…'

'Is anything hurting?' Kelly asked. 'Apart from your contractions?'

'My foot. Ankle. Or it was… It's kind of numb now but I can't get it out.'

Ari leaned closer, stretching one arm into the footwell and keeping the torch in his other hand to try and see what he was doing. The driver's door was badly crumpled inwards and the accelerator and brake pedals were bent and pressed onto Zoe's foot. A brief attempt was all it took for Ari to realise that specialised equipment would be needed to free Zoe. And it was needed soon. There was icy water swirling around those pedals as well. The passenger side doors were well above water level at the moment but it was seeping in on the lower side.

Kelly had the kit open on the back seat beside her. She pushed a blood-pressure cuff and a stethoscope between the front seats.

'Can you get a blood pressure?'

'Sure.' Ari already had his hand on Zoe's wrist. 'Heart rate's one hundred and five. And the pulse is strong so she's not hypotensive. I'll get an accurate blood pressure in a minute. There's a Doppler in that kit, too, isn't there? I'd like to check on baby's heart rate.'

'I'll get it.'

'Tell me about your pregnancy, Zoe,' Ari said. 'Is it your first? Have you had any problems?'

But Zoe didn't answer. She reached out and clutched his hand as she screwed up her face again and cried out. 'This hurts *so* much...'

'We'll get you some pain relief,' Kelly said. 'How long since that last contraction, Ari?'

'Between two and three minutes at a guess.' He glanced at his watch. 'I'll keep time for the frequency and duration.'

'Here…' Kelly handed a methoxyflurane inhaler between the seats moments later. 'It's got the activated carbon chamber inserted and the cap off. Put the loop over Zoe's wrist so it doesn't get dropped.'

There was no point in checking for contra-indications or trying to coach Zoe into using the inhaled analgesic until her contraction was over. Ari also needed to examine Zoe to see if delivery was imminent. With a bit of luck, they might be able to get her into the ambulance before that happened. Above them, from the direction of the road on the broken side of the bridge, he could see more flashing lights and hear people shouting. It seemed the fire service was now on scene with their heavy vehicles and ability to not only stabilise a car in a precarious situation but to cut through and bend metal to make extrication possible.

Ari was able to get a blood-pressure reading as Zoe's pain ebbed. 'One-forty on ninety,' he relayed to Kelly. They both knew it was the high end of normal but that was hardly surprising given the circumstances and level of anxiety. 'Can you try and release the lever on the other side of Zoe's seat? If we could tilt her back a bit, it'll make it much easier for me to find out what this baby's up to.'

'I'm not having this baby here,' Zoe said. 'I can't... What if...? *Ahh...*' This time it was a cry of fear rather than pain and Ari thought he heard an echo of the same sound from Kelly as the car suddenly shifted, scraping over boulders on the creek bed beneath them and tilting down more sharply on the driver's side.

'It's okay,' Ari told them. 'Look...the firefighters are putting a hook on the back of the car. It's only moved because they're making sure it's secure and it can't float away. We're safe... I'm not going to let anything bad happen, okay?'

His words were intended as reassurance for their patient but he knew they were still in a very dangerous situation—even more so, if that hook didn't have a good grip on the chassis of the car. Kelly had to know that as well but, when Ari turned his head to check that she was all right, he could see that she was also hanging onto his words so he held her gaze for a heartbeat longer. So that she would know he meant what he said and that Kelly was included in his protection.

He wasn't going to let anything bad happen to her—not if there was any way he could possibly prevent it. The urge to protect Kelly was so strong, in fact, that Ari could feel it snatch his own breath for a moment. Had he made a mistake in encouraging her to get to Zoe before the vehicle had been stabilised? Taken advantage of that extraordinary courage she displayed because he wanted her by his side in this challenge? No…she'd been just as determined as he'd been, hadn't she? That determination to help others was one of the traits they had in common. One that, right from the start, had created that connection but right now it felt like more than simply being members of the same team. It felt like a bond that was soul-deep. They were in this together and it just felt…right…

As if they'd done this many times before. As if they would keep doing it, perhaps for the rest of their lives. An unbreakable team. Soul-mates…

* * *

How on earth had she ended up in what had to be the most dangerous situation she'd ever faced in her career? There was water covering Kelly's feet now and the car was beginning to rock in the increasing current of the flood waters. The splashes combined with the heavy rain coming through the open door beside her and she could feel it trickling beneath her raincoat to soak her scrub suit and chill her whole body.

What was even more extraordinary, mind you, was that she could feel she was actually quite safe as long as Ari was there. And somewhere in the back of her mind, as she reached for the lever to try and flatten the back of the driver's seat, was the knowledge that even if the worst happened and this car got washed away, she knew that she wouldn't willingly be abandoning Zoe, even if it was to try and save her own life. Because she knew that it wouldn't even occur to Ari to do that?

She could hear him explain to Zoe how to use the inhaler for pain relief when her next contraction started and, although his voice was muted by the sound of water rushing past and fire officers getting closer to the vehicle and shouting instructions as they brought heavy equipment down the bank, just the calmness of that rumble of his voice was enough to reassure Kelly that he was in control. That *they* were in control of managing their patient, at least. The seat mechanism was still working and Kelly had pulled the back down as far as she could.

'Okay, Zoe, breathe in through the inhaler…hold it…keep holding…now breathe out, still through the inhaler. Kelly? Can I have some fresh gloves, please?'

'Sure.' She found the large-sized gloves in the kit. 'Do you want the Doppler now?'

His hand covered hers as he reached for the gloves and the brief glance told her that there might be more urgent things to do than find out the baby's heart rate. A fire officer was leaning in the open side of the car as Ari pulled on the gloves.

'We're going to break the window on the driver's side,' he told them, 'so we can get that door off and get the patient free. I'm going to put this sheet of plastic over you all to keep you safe from the glass, okay?'

'Okay.' Kelly answered for them both. Ari was busy talking to Zoe.

'I need to check what's happening down below as soon as this contraction is over, Zoe.'

Zoe pulled the inhaler from her mouth. 'I can feel something,' she groaned. 'I need to push...'

'Hang on. Try not to push just yet. Pant for me, sweetheart. Or blow, like there's lot of candles on that cake and you want them all to flicker.'

Somehow, Ari was twisting his big body so that he could reach between Zoe's legs at the same time as the plastic sheet was being stuffed into the interior of the car and Kelly was helping to pull it over them.

And then...there they were. The three of them very close together inside a strange plastic tent. There was thumping and crashing outside and the sound of breaking glass and the noise of pneumatic tools starting up but it faded into the background as Kelly leaned over Zoe's head, holding a torch to try and give Ari some light.

'I can feel baby's head,' he told Zoe. 'Let's see if we can get you into a better position and then you can push on your next contraction.'

There was no way Zoe could move her

trapped foot but she was able to bend her other leg.

'I don't want to push,' she sobbed. 'I don't want to have my baby here. Get me out... *please*...get me out of here...'

'It's okay, Zoe.' Ari had his mouth close to his patient's ear. 'We're here with you. Your baby wants to come now and it's okay. We've got this. *You've* got this...'

He caught Kelly's gaze for a second. He didn't need to tell her that there was a limited time to deliver this baby safely now that it was already this far on its way. Even if the fire service got the door off in the next minute or two and could bend metal enough to free Zoe's foot, they weren't going to be moving her anywhere until this baby was born. Kelly squeezed through more of the gap between the seats to get close enough to hold Zoe's hand and try and help encourage her as her next contraction began.

'You can do this, Zoe. We've got you.' The grip on her hand was crushing her fingers but Kelly barely noticed. 'That's it...you're doing great.' With her other hand she was still holding the torch to provide some light for Ari.

'Push, Zoe.' Ari's voice was command-

ing. 'That's it. Good girl… Keep it going…
push…push…*push…*'

'I…*can't*,' Zoe gasped. 'It's too hard…
it's… *Ahh…*'

'You're almost there. One more push…'

'As hard as you can,' Kelly urged. In the
spotlight from the torch, she could see the baby's head between Zoe's legs, between Ari's
hands as he supported the infant and gently
tilted its body to help deliver the first shoulder. And then, with another, sharp cry from
Zoe, it was over in a rush, with Ari managing to catch the slippery bundle before it
could get anywhere near the water that had
risen almost to the level of the seats as the
door was being prised off this side of the car.

They were still all inside the plastic co-
coon as Ari lifted the baby whose first cry
cut through the cacophony of noise from outside the tent as access was gained to deal
with the pedals trapping Zoe's foot. Kelly
had to move now. To find what they needed
to cut the umbilical cord and what she had
that she could cover the infant with to prevent hypothermia. And then they needed to
get him to a safe space as fast as possible but,
for a heartbeat, she was caught by the look
on Ari's face.

A lot of what she could read in his expression was reflecting the same relief that she was feeling—that the baby *was* crying and not in need of resuscitation in an impossible setting but she could see much more than that in his eyes as well. The whole miracle of birth was amazing enough in any circumstances but to snatch a victory in what could have been a disastrous situation was…well… it was overwhelming enough to bring the prickle of tears to the back of her own eyes. Kelly was never going to forget this moment. Or the way Ari was looking at her right now. As if they had been a team forever and nothing was going to break that bond of trust.

For a heartbeat, Kelly actually believed that she could return that trust. That it might be possible to recapture that dream she'd once had of finding a person that she could trust—and love—enough to want to spend the rest of her life with them, and it was something that she wanted to believe so much that it hurt. But this was not the time to allow what was an emotion rather than a coherent thought any more than that tiny blink of time.

Already, Kelly was turning away, the conscious part of her brain listing the items like the clamps and sterile scissors and foil survival sheets that she needed to locate in the kit. It was time to cut this baby's umbilical cord and wrap it up to carry to a safe, warm place where they could complete an accurate Apgar score and check that all was well. It would only be moments before Zoe could also be lifted from the car and carried to the warmth of the ambulance for a proper assessment and transport to hospital, probably with the third stage of her labour happening en route.

Maybe later—much later when the chaos of this call out had finally been sorted—she might get drawn back to that moment and find that it would be only too easy to conjure up that sense of longing for a lost dream again. Or maybe it would be better to simply leave it where it was, as part of an extraordinary, once-in-a-lifetime experience that would never happen again.

Like holding this newborn baby in her arms, wrapped up in the foil sheet, as firemen reached in through the open doors to take the kit out of the way and then help her out of the vehicle and up the bank to safety. At the same time, more rescuers were lifting Zoe from the car. As Kelly made sure she had a secure grip on the precious bundle she was holding as someone draped a blanket around them, a quick glance over her shoulder showed her that Zoe was now in Ari's arms. He was standing knee deep in the swirling, icy water of the stream and his head was bent so that his mouth was close to Zoe's ear, as if he was saying something he wanted only her to hear. It must have been something reassuring, Kelly thought, judging by the way Zoe wrapped her arms around his neck and tucked her head beneath his shoulder and against his chest—as if she'd found the safest place in the world.

Or maybe that was how anybody would feel once they were in the circle of those arms? Kelly shook the notion away almost as quickly as it surfaced. Errant thoughts, imagining what it might be like to be a lot closer to Ari Lawson than was appropriate for a colleague—even one who was a good friend—were becoming a bit of a habit. A bad habit that had the potential to undermine her focus on her work. It only took a shift of her glance to the tiny face visible in the crook of her elbow to regain that focus and the pressure of supporting hands on each side

of her was, quite literally, another step in the
right direction.

'Let's go, baby,' she whispered. 'We've got
this…'

of her was quite literally another step in the right direction.

'Looks OK,' she said. 'We've got this.'

CHAPTER SEVEN

'IT'S NOT BROKEN.' The orthopaedic registrar was staring intently at the computer screen where the X-ray of Zoe's ankle was illuminated. 'Looks like just some bad bruising.'

Ari caught Kelly's glance. 'Exactly what you thought,' he murmured.

There was a glow of satisfaction in her eyes. 'Had to get an X-ray to be sure, though. How's that paperwork going?'

'Almost done.'

Ari was adding the clinical description of his part in Zoe's rescue and the birth of her baby to their report, including the third stage with the delivery of the placenta that had happened as they'd travelled back to hospital with Zoe in the second ambulance, which had had both a stretcher and baby carrier available. Her baby had been well enough to travel with the new mother, having not needed the incubator in the flying squad's ambulance.

They were in one corner of the larger resus room that had been ready for Zoe on arrival at the Kensington and, until a few minutes ago, it had been a crowded space. Members of the obstetric team on call had joined the emergency department staff, paged to check that there were no complications from Zoe's dramatic labour under such challenging conditions, but apart from a minor tear, it appeared that all was well. The paediatrician who had also been paged had been quite happy with the condition of the baby, who was now cradled in Zoe's arms, sound asleep after all the excitement.

Bruce, the volunteer driver for the flying squad, had come to tell Kelly and Ari that the squad's ambulance was cleaned up and ready for a new crew and that he was heading home with their shift done and dusted. A police officer had also come in not long ago to tell Zoe that they had managed to contact both her husband and her parents and they were all on their way to see her.

'I'm pretty much done with the paperwork, too.' Kelly pushed back a strand of her hair that had come loose. 'Did you know that there are reporters waiting outside and a television news crew? They've already got pictures of the scene and some of the story from the police but they'd like to talk to us before they come in to get an interview with Zoe and some close-ups of the baby.' She grinned at Ari. 'We might be a little bit famous.'

'It's the kind of story everybody loves, I guess.' Ari signed the bottom of the patient report form. 'Some real drama and danger and not just a happy ending but a cute baby as well.'

The kind of story that Ari knew would be a career highlight and one that he would remember for the rest of his life. And, professionally speaking, it had been an experience that only he and Kelly would ever share. Nobody else could ever truly understand the flash of fear that had come with the scrape and rock of the car shifting on the rocks, with them both knowing that if it got washed away it was quite possible that neither of them would survive. And nobody else could relate to that astonishing wash of relief on hearing Zoe's baby cry for the first time because it could only have been that intense due to the unusual combination of factors—not just the danger and the tension but the fact that he and Kelly had been working so closely together under that plastic tent.

That bond of being a team that Ari had been aware of as they'd started that job had strengthened tenfold now and, even though his clothing was still damp enough to be chilling his body and he had mud splatters from head to foot, including in his hair, he wasn't in any hurry to leave this room. Or perhaps it was Kelly's company he didn't want to leave because he didn't want to break this new bond. Or to turn his back on the kind of glow that Kelly had right now—the kind that advertised the confidence and satisfaction of an exceptionally challenging job well done.

The kind of glow that Ari would want her to have as often as possible because it meant that she was happy with who she was. Proud of herself—as she should be. He would prefer to make sure that it would be remembered so well that Kelly could tap into it if—or probably when—she had moments when she doubted her own self-worth. Like maybe the next time her path crossed that of the bastard of an ex-boyfriend and he tried to put her down again.

When they'd said goodbye to Zoe, brushed off her heartfelt thanks and admired the baby again, they slipped out of the resus room. They had a choice of whether to head for the locker room, where they'd left their personal items like street clothing this morning, or to go to the waiting area where they knew the reporters had gathered.

'You were amazing out there.' Ari paused to nod towards the doors that led to the waiting room. 'You deserve to be more than a little bit famous.'

'You were the real hero. I think I'd rather have a hot shower and some dinner.'

'Oh…you and me both. I'd better text Stacey and see if she wants me to bring takeaway home.' He pulled out his phone and started tapping even as he kept talking. 'I'd like to pop in on Peggy but I can't go anywhere like this and by the time I've been home and cleaned up, it'll be too late to come back.'

'You could shower here.' But Kelly was staring at Ari's head as they moved, by tacit consent, towards the locker room. 'How did you get so much mud in your *hair*? I think you'll need some heavy-duty shampoo rather than just soap.'

Ari's phone buzzed. 'I don't need to take food home,' he told Kelly. 'Apparently Stacey has a friend visiting and they're making cheese toasties. Hey…why don't we both shower here and go across to the pub? Being almost famous calls for a celebration, doesn't it?'

'I'd rather use my own shower,' Kelly said. 'I'm only down the road a bit. Ten minutes' walk at the most.' Ahead of Ari as they reached the locker room, she turned to glance over her shoulder. 'You could come too, if you like. I'm sure I've got a beer lurking in the back of the fridge behind some wine and there's the best Chinese takeaway almost next door. That way you'd still be close enough to go and see Peggy before you head home.'

There was no reason to take Kelly up on her offer, given that there was a shower available in the locker room and he could find something to eat across the road.

But there was every reason to take up her offer, because it meant that he could put off breaking that new bond with Kelly for a bit longer. Plus, he had to admit he was curious to see where Kelly lived and get more of a glimpse into her private life. That curiosity along with the undeniable reluctance to leave her company won any internal debate with ease.

'Can we take my bike? I've got a spare helmet in a pannier and that way I can be somewhere else in a hurry if I need to.'

'Sure.'

Kelly's smile assured him that it was no big deal but was the slight hesitation he'd been aware of before her answer and the way her glance slid away from his trying to tell him something else? That maybe he'd made the wrong choice here? That he was taking a new turn on a pathway that might be impossible to undo? He brushed the warning off as irrelevant until he was standing very close to Kelly a short time later, his fingers brushing the soft skin beneath her chin when he was helping her fasten the strap of the helmet.

Oh, *man*… Had he ever felt a tingle of awareness quite like that when he'd touched a woman's skin? He didn't dare catch Kelly's gaze because he didn't want her to see any hint of what he was feeling. Instead, he drew in a slow breath and slammed internal doors on that tingle and any significance it might have. He couldn't—*wouldn't*—go there. For both their sakes. A bit of self-discipline was all that was needed here and exerting that kind of self-control had never been a problem for Ari.

'Have you been on a bike before?'

Kelly shook her head.

'You don't need to do anything except hang on. Best if you put your arms around my waist.'

Best for safety, anyway. It might not be quite such a good thought when it came to that self-control, Ari decided when he felt Kelly's arms tighten around his waist and her body pressing against his back but, somewhat to his surprise, it actually helped. By the time he had parked his bike by the steps that led down to Kelly's basement flat, being so close that they were physically touching each other was feeling familiar. No different from any friend he might have offered a motorbike ride to.

Something had changed.

Something big…

Kelly wasn't quite sure what it was but she knew it had happened because of how dangerous that mission to help Zoe and her baby had been. Because circumstances had pushed her and Ari to work alone together in a life-and-death situation. An oddly intimate situation at the most crucial point, in fact, because they'd been cut off from even the rest of the rescue effort by that thick plastic sheeting.

Whatever alchemy had occurred, it had certainly brought them closer together. So close that Kelly knew they were treading the very fine line that could lie between friendship and something a whole lot more significant. It was the same kind of tension that she'd been aware of the other day, when they'd been waiting for Peggy to come out of surgery and she'd been so sure that Ari had been about to kiss her. And, because this wasn't the first time, it didn't make her feel nearly so wary. When Ari's fingers brushed the skin of her neck as he was doing up her helmet, Kelly could feel the buzz of tension as something pleasurable rather than a warning.

Something even more pleasurable than standing in her hot shower now, rinsing away both soap suds and some of the chill of that flooded stream. Ari had insisted that she have the first shower and Kelly had agreed because she didn't need to wash her hair immediately so she could be quicker. Ari was choosing something from the takeout menu for the nearby Chinese restaurant and placing the order while she was in the bathroom and Kelly was going to go and pick up the food while he was having his turn in the shower.

By the time she got back, the gas fire should have done its job to make her small sitting room that doubled as a dining room cosy enough to make them both forget the less pleasant aspects of that damp and muddy mission and, if he was as hungry as she was, the food would be even more welcome.

Kelly couldn't wait. She turned off the shower, hurriedly towelled herself dry and then dressed in her favourite "at home" clothes of her most comfortable yoga pants, an oversized sweatshirt and some old sheepskin boots. She pulled her hair out of its bun and brushed it but didn't bother tying it up again. She wanted to make sure that Ari didn't interpret this invitation to come home with her as anything other than casual. Convenient. The kind of thing that any friends could do and no reason at all to run. Or hide. Those boundaries were still visible and they wouldn't be crossed. Not unless that was a mutual choice.

'Shower's all yours,' she told Ari as she

grabbed her shoulder bag on her way through living room to the front door. 'And help yourself to a beer from the fridge. I'll be back with dinner in no time.'

Being the end of the weekend, however, the takeout section of the popular local restaurant was being well patronised and it took longer than Kelly had expected. It was raining again as she came out into the dark of the early evening and gusts of wind were picking up long tresses of her hair to make them tangle around her face. Fortunately, it didn't take long to get home and down the steps to let herself back into the flat, with her bag full of cardboard boxes of steaming rice and fragrant food.

'Wow...that smells amazing.'

Ari's voice came from behind Kelly as she pushed the door shut and she turned to see him coming out of the bathroom, rubbing at his head with a towel. The only clothing he had on was a pair of faded jeans and, while they were zipped up, the top button hadn't yet been fastened. Maybe that was what undid something deep inside Kelly and unleashed a shaft of desire that made her breath catch in astonishment. Or maybe it was Ari dropping the towel around his shoulders to reveal that his hair—that Kelly had only seen sleeked back into a tidy man bun—was loose and falling in soft, damp waves to frame his face and neck.

That little gas fire had certainly done its job in warming this room up. Kelly was suddenly feeling overheated. Because she'd come back in from being out in a cold, rainy evening? No. It didn't take more than a split second to realise that this heat had very little to do with any external source. No wonder people who were good looking were described as being "hot". Kelly was melting right now because she'd never seen anyone who was as beautiful as Ari Lawson was at this moment.

This small room was making him seem taller. Broader. Or perhaps it was because Kelly could see *so* much of that smooth, olive skin covering muscles that her fingers itched to touch the shape of. He looked so different with his hair loose as well. Softer? Or was that impression due to how dark his eyes seemed in the shadows of that tousled hair?

Whatever the reason, Kelly was still having trouble catching her breath. She was still aware of that spear of sensation that was a white heat deep in her belly and there were tendrils of that heat reaching her toes and fingertips to make them also feel as if they were melting. Losing their function anyway, because the handle of the bag Kelly was holding slipped from her fingers to land on the floorboards.

'Oh, *no…*' Kelly dropped to a crouch. 'I'm so clumsy…'

'Oops…' Ari swooped at the same time to rescue the bag.

The waxed boxes were sealed tightly enough not to have spilled their contents but they were falling out of the top of the bag and both Ari and Kelly reached for them at the same time so that what actually happened was that Ari caught hold of Kelly's hand instead of a box.

Time appeared to stop in that instant. Kelly lifted her gaze but then froze as it met Ari's. She felt her pulse suddenly speed up and then trip as it missed a beat but it was the only part of her body that was moving. Even her lungs had given up on the idea of drawing in a fresh breath.

Oh…*my…* Kelly completely forgot about the food she'd been about to rescue. She couldn't even smell it now because she was close enough to Ari to be able to smell the shampoo and soap he'd been using. *Her* shampoo and soap, which made the scent familiar enough to feel safe but, mixed with the background musk of potent masculinity, it was different enough to be arousing her senses in a way that was making everything completely new—brilliantly clear and so sharp and bright it was as if she was using those senses properly for the first time in her life. And, because time had stopped, she was aware of every one of them.

That touch of his hand on her own, almost burning her skin with the intensity of the sensation. Kelly could feel the puff of his breath on her face at the same time because they were that close and she could hear it as a sigh. She could feel the warmth of that breath as well—or was it the heat that seemed to be radiating from his skin? Her gaze finally drifted down to his lips, having torn itself away from the depths of those wickedly dark eyes that she just knew could see every single thing she was thinking and feeling.

Taste… That was the only sense that Kelly wasn't using but, somehow, she knew how delicious it would be to put her tongue against that gorgeous, olive skin. Or to lose herself in a kiss that would totally capture her mouth. Unconsciously, the tip of her tongue came out to dampen her bottom lip as she imagined that kiss and it was then that she heard the change in that breath that Ari was releasing. An almost sound that—if it had involved his vocal cords—could have been a groan of desire. Of lust even...

How could so many impressions and the flash of so many thoughts happen with such speed? There was a warning sounding somewhere in the back of Kelly's mind—something to do with what she'd been told about Ari and how women never stayed long in his life. But at that same instant Kelly had the feeling that those women wouldn't have regretted being there when they looked back, no matter how short the time had been, because they would have shared something very special. As unique as Ari was. She would settle for whatever he wanted to offer her at this moment, even if that was no more than a kiss. Because everything had changed. Or maybe it was only one thing that had changed but that one thing had the power to change the rest of her life.

It wasn't simply the familiar scent of her own toiletries on Ari's skin and hair that were providing a sense of safety, was it?

That had been there well before she'd even invited Ari into her home. It had been there at that moment when she'd become aware of that new bond between herself and Ari when they'd heard Zoe's baby cry for the first time and they'd become a real team. A partnership that could accomplish more than either of them could on their own. People who could totally trust each other.

And Kelly had been aware that there was something even bigger than anything professional in knowing that she *could* trust Ari. For a split second she'd known that it might just be possible to go back in time— or at least reset something in her heart or her head that would allow her to trust in someone enough to believe that they would never set out to hurt her. That the dream of finding someone who would be a partner for life might not have vanished for ever.

Her breath had already caught in her throat and now there was a squeeze in her chest that meant she wouldn't be trying to use her lungs anytime too soon. A squeeze that was tight enough to be painful, as Kelly understood that she had already given that trust to Ari without realising that she had. How could she not have known when she'd recognised the danger they'd been in in that car and yet she'd felt safe because she'd had Ari by her side?

She could feel that internal squeeze morphing into something else. Something that was just between herself and Ari and, yes, it had a lot to do with wanting him and the need to touch and be touched, but it there was more to it than simply sex. There was something huge happening here that had the potential to be as full of hope—and joy—as the safe arrival of Zoe's baby had been.

It could only have been enough time for a few heartbeats since they'd both dropped to reach for that bag at the same time but it felt like for ever. Enough time for so much to fall into place for Kelly anyway. And enough time for a silent conversation to have happened. For questions to be asked and answered. For desire to be acknowledged and permission given to explore it, at least a little.

And, still, Kelly hadn't taken a new breath but it didn't seem to matter. She had to close her eyes against the intensity of what she could see in Ari's eyes as he closed the gap between their faces in the same kind of slow motion that the last seconds had been played out in. She wanted to let her eyes drift shut anyway, because all she wanted to do right now was to feel. And taste…

This wasn't supposed to be happening.

Okay, he'd had that warning that he was a little too aware of Kelly as more than a colleague or a friend but he'd been so confident that he could keep his distance enough to make sure nothing got out of control.

But here he was—a heartbeat away from kissing Kelly Reynolds. *Again*… Knowing that it was exactly what she wanted as much as he did. And maybe she needed it to happen far more than he needed it *not* to happen? Right from that first time he'd met Kelly— when he'd seen her confidence and courage shrink before his eyes when she had been faced by that idiot of an ex-boyfriend—he'd sensed that she needed someone to make it obvious how incredibly special she was and give her the confidence to believe in herself, no matter what situation she might find herself in in the future. How much easier would it be to communicate that with a kiss than by trying to find the words that would be convincing enough?

He'd known all along that he didn't have the space in his life for someone like Kelly—

that it wouldn't be fair on anyone involved to indulge in his usual kind of short-term fling and that he could never consider anything long term—but he'd also known that the pull might prove to be irresistible. And he wasn't the only one who could feel that pull from Kelly, was he? A brief encounter with Stacey had been enough for his foster sister to make a real attempt to change aspects of her life and Peggy...well, Peggy had been captured by that very first meeting with Kelly. Or perhaps she had sensed a connection that was already there between Ari and Kelly that neither of them had recognised.

'You're just the sort of girl who'd be perfect for my Ari...'

The boundaries had been there, though, despite any attraction and that near miss in the waiting room the other day. They both had their reasons for keeping the boundaries intact. Ari had never wanted to find a "serious" relationship with anyone and Kelly had clearly had her trust in so many things damaged. In men, relationships and, worst of all, in herself. But something had changed today.

It had changed at that moment when the car had lurched and scraped on those rocks and he'd conquered his own fear in order to try and reassure both Zoe and Kelly. When he'd promised he was not going to let anything bad happen to them. When he'd held Kelly's gaze to make sure she knew that he meant what he said. Even now, Ari could still feel how strong that urge to protect her had been and it wasn't just that he wanted to keep her safe from physical harm. He knew perfectly well that emotional harm could have even more far-reaching effects and he also knew that there was a new connection that had been cemented between himself and Kelly today. A connection that was, possibly, as deep as any connection between two people could be.

Trust.

A form of love all on its own and perhaps the first real trust Kelly could believe in for a very long time. A first, huge step towards healing? Ari could sense that if he pushed back from Kelly now, as her eyes were drifting shut, he would be breaking this promise of a kiss that was hanging in the air between them, and that would mean he would somehow be breaking that trust as well.

He couldn't do that.

Besides… Ari could feel the relief as he relaxed his muscles enough to allow him to lean forward and touch Kelly's lips with his own. It was only going to be a kiss after all.

Just a kiss.

What harm could that do?

CHAPTER EIGHT

'Oh, no… I thought Stacey or Ari would be able to answer the door. I didn't want you to have to get up.'

'I'm fine, lovey. Getting better every day. Come in…' Peggy turned to lead the way towards the kitchen at the back of her house. 'Ari's just popped out to collect Stace. She had an outing with her antenatal group today—it's a special one for teenage mothers and I think they went to visit a play centre.'

Peggy was using a walking stick and moving slowly and carefully but, when she turned to smile at Kelly at the kitchen door, there was no sign of her being in too much pain. If anything, she looked much happier than when Kelly had last seen her in hospital a week or so ago.

'I've been telling Ari that I'm quite ready for visitors now. Especially *you*…' Her smile was making the crinkles around her eyes deeper. 'Did you bring your squares?'

'I did. I think I've made enough of them to start joining some up. It's a bit addictive, isn't it? Knitting? People are laughing at me at work because I take it out when things are quiet.'

'I've always found it very soothing, I have to say.' Peggy nodded.

She was making her way to the old couch at the far end of the huge kitchen which was draped with one of the colourful, handmade blankets that Kelly was currently aspiring to create. Kelly offered her a supportive arm as she settled and then put her feet up and, as she did so, she remembered the first time she had ever been in this room and had a clear memory of how tenderly Ari had settled his foster mum onto these cushions and how his touch could reveal how much he loved someone. The memory gave her one of those chest-tightening moments that felt like one's heart was being held in a hand that could squeeze so hard it brought tears to your eyes.

Because she now knew just how tender Ari was capable of being. What the touch of his hands was actually like and how incredibly special it could make you feel. It *could* make you feel genuinely loved, although Kelly was trying to remind herself that it was simply sex and didn't necessarily mean anything more than the fact they were so attracted to each other. The first time had been a revelation, mind you. And the second time, only days ago, had been even more astonishing, so there was something snapping at the heels of that tenderness that made a lot more than her heart feel a squeeze.

Kelly might be getting used to these sensations of pure desire that could be conjured up with no more than a thought about Ari Lawson and create a delicious knot deep in her belly but it didn't make them any less powerful. If anything, they were getting stronger. Strong enough to make her close her eyes as she took a breath and rode the wave of that knot tightening to the point of pain and then ebbing to leave a delicious tingle. It happened even if he wasn't anywhere nearby or she couldn't even hear his voice on a phone call or something.

When he *was* breathing the same air, it took only the briefest eye contact for the need to be alone with him to become almost overpowering but, on the plus side, they were already learning that it could build a tension that could take sex to the next level. To a level that Kelly hadn't ever guessed even existed, in fact.

'Pop the kettle on, there's a love.' Peggy settled back on her cushions with a sigh. 'I'm a bit parched and it's past time for afternoon tea.'

'Do you need anything else? Painkillers maybe?'

'No, thanks, lovey. I'm good. Just pass me that bag of wool over there and I'll see what I can find to edge your squares. A dark colour is usually best. Have you ever done any crochet?'

'No.' Kelly's heart sank. 'I've seen people doing it and it looks harder than knitting.'

'It's easier,' Peggy said. 'You don't have to do an edging—you can just sew the squares together but I think it looks better. Like this...' She traced the dark outline on the squares of the blanket hanging beside her over the back of the couch. 'I think it brings everything together and makes it perfect.'

About to agree, Kelly was distracted by the sound of people arriving as the front door slammed shut. The ripple of laughter made her catch Peggy's gaze in surprise because she'd never heard Stacey laughing before. And then her own lips were curving into a smile as she heard the answering rumble of Ari's laughter and she couldn't look away from the door because she couldn't wait to see him again. To feel that squeeze in her belly and the warmth of a pleasure—so deep it was indescribable—that she knew would touch every cell in her body the instant that Ari's gaze met her own.

And...there it was. Still smiling, Kelly moved to get on with the task of making a pot of tea. Peggy's attention was on Stacey now as the teenager went straight towards her, clearly eager to tell her about the class visit, so the opportunity to agree with her about how those dark edges drew the squares of a blanket together had passed. But Kelly couldn't have agreed more. She caught Ari's gaze again, briefly, on her way to putting the kettle on. Having him back home with Peggy and Stacey and having herself included in this family group had brought things together as well. And it did feel perfect. For now, at least.

And, okay...she knew that it probably wasn't going to go anywhere. Ari was only planning to be in London for as long as

Peggy needed him and he didn't do long-term relationships anyway but…but when he made love to her, it *felt* like there was a lot more to it than simply sex. That maybe Ari was falling in love with her even if he didn't realise it himself or believe that it was something that could last.

The voices behind her were just a background murmur.

'You should have seen Stace at the play centre, Ma. She's a natural. I've got a photo of her with a bunch of the kids. I'm going to print it out and put it on the corkboard.'

'They told us there are certificates you can get to be a childcare worker. I reckon I could do that one day.'

'Of course you could, lovey. We'll find out about it, shall we?'

With the kettle full, Kelly flicked the switch to boil the water and opened a cupboard to find cups and saucers. She felt her breath escaping in a long sigh. No matter how perfect things felt right now, she wasn't sure she herself believed that what she and Ari had found together was going to last. What was that saying? Oh, yeah… If something seemed too good to be true, it probably was…

* * *

This was shaping up to be a really good day, Ari decided as he cleared up the cups and plates from their afternoon tea.

Peggy was looking the best she had since she'd been discharged from hospital. Better than she'd looked since he'd come back to London, that was for sure. Maybe the surgery she had gone through was going to buy enough time for her to not only see Stacey's baby arrive but to know that the young mother was going to be okay and have a future to look forward to, even if Peggy wasn't here to support and encourage her.

Even better than the positive things happening at home was the fact that Kelly was visiting this afternoon. Ari had loved this house for almost as long as he could remember. When he'd finally learned that he was safe here, there was nothing he'd loved more than coming through that red front door, knowing that he belonged here. That it was *home*. And Kelly somehow just fitted right in as if she belonged here, too. It had, in fact, seemed like that even the first time she'd stepped through that red door and she'd been so gentle and caring in the way she'd treated Peggy.

His mum…

She'd been here since then, of course, for that dinner that Peggy had insisted he invite her to. Right now, she was sitting on a footstool beside the couch and the glow of her blonde hair was almost touching the silver of Peggy's curls as they bent over something they were doing with those knitted squares that Kelly was so proud of. Her hair was loose again today and Ari's fingers itched to lace themselves through those waves. The way he had that first time he'd kissed her.

For a second, his breath caught in his chest as his body reminded him of what it was like to kiss Kelly. Had he really believed that it was ever going to be "just a kiss"? How could any man have resisted the overpowering urge to go further when it was like nothing he'd ever experienced before and the invitation had been there so clearly it had felt like he was responding to a need more than simply a desire.

Maybe it had been a need on both sides. To remind Kelly to believe in herself and that she deserved everything she wanted in her future, and for him perhaps it had been a release that he hadn't realised he'd needed so badly. He'd come to London because his beloved foster mother was dying and the prospect of a life ending was a background sadness to everything else that was happening. Making love with Kelly had reminded him that life was for living as well. That there was magic to be found in not being alone sometimes.

Maybe the feeling that Kelly belonged here, in this house, wasn't because she'd been here before or because she got on so well with Peggy. Maybe it was because she actually belonged with *him*…

The longing that came with that idea was disturbing enough to make Ari abandon the washing up and head out of the kitchen to give himself a bit of space. He had a good reason to go, anyway, because he'd told Peggy he was going to print off the nice photo of Stacey with the toddlers at the play centre. He went into an office where he could download the photos from his phone to the printer but the task wasn't complex enough to distract him completely. He could actually feel an internal battle kicking off.

He *wanted* to believe that he could find someone like Kelly and imagine a perfect future where he had his own house and a family to come home to every day. But he knew that reality could be very, very different and he'd learned long ago that it was safer to assume that good things never lasted because then you wouldn't get crushed when they ended. The lessons learned in how to protect himself—and others—were so deeply engrained they felt like they were part of his DNA so it was quite possible that he would never be able to make himself vulnerable by trusting someone else with something as important as his own future. His own heart.

But the longing was there, wasn't it?

And the strength of it was a warning all by itself.

Holding the printed photo in his hand was a tangible reminder of the reasons he was here in the first place. For Peggy and, because she was so anxious about Stacey, it was of the greatest importance to do whatever he could to sort things for his foster sister as well. They had to be his priority, which made it easy to push aside any wants or needs that were purely personal. And that was a relief because it meant that he didn't have to think about it any more, which only stirred up stuff that was better left back in a past that was so distant it was irrelevant.

'Hey Stace…' He paused by her bedroom

door because he could see her feet, which meant she was lounging on her bed. 'Want to see the photo again? It's a belter.'

'Maybe later.'

Something in her tone made Ari pause and peer around the edge of her door. In her favourite purple dungarees, she still didn't look hugely pregnant, especially when she was curled up like that, leaning back on her pillows as she stared at her phone, texting rapidly.

'Everything okay?'

'Yeah…' The tone was aggressive. 'Why wouldn't it be?'

Ari backed off so as not to antagonise Stacey any further but he knew he was frowning as he entered the kitchen again. Something was going on there and his instinct told him he might not like what it was.

Peggy was delighted to see the photo. So was Kelly.

'She looks so happy,' Kelly said.

'I think it would be brilliant if she could work with children.' Peggy nodded. 'I'd forgotten how good she used to be with the littlies, like Ari was. She might even want to become a teacher one day. I'll have to see if she could catch up on her GSCEs at night school or something—while I'm around to help look after the baby.'

Both Ari and Kelly made encouraging murmurs but she caught his gaze for a heartbeat. Peggy's surgeon had been very pleased with how her surgery had gone and her oncologist had said they could hope for a better quality of life but nobody wanted to say how long Peggy might still have and, unless a small miracle got pulled out of the bag, it was possible it wasn't going to be more than a few months.

'I'll put it on the corkboard.'

Kelly followed him, carrying a teacup that had he'd forgotten to collect earlier. 'I should probably head home. I think I've got the hang of crochet enough to be going on with.'

'No, no...' Peggy shook her head. 'Stay for dinner. We'd love to have you. If you don't mind leftovers, that is.'

'I don't want to make any more work for anybody,' Kelly said firmly. 'And I've got some work to catch up on.' She paused to look at the corkboard as she went past. 'Oh, my God... Is that *you*, Ari?'

'Yeah... I know. But dreadlocks seemed cool at the time. To be fair, I was only seventeen.'

Kelly's grin faded as she looked up. 'And is that baby you're holding Stacey?'

'I guess it must be.'

'It was indeed,' Peggy said. 'It was when she started pulling on those awful dreadlocks that he decided it was time to cut them off—and thank goodness for that.'

Kelly was smiling again, holding his gaze, and Ari could see so much in those gorgeous blue eyes. An appreciation for his love of babies and respect for him going against convention and devoting his career to the most vulnerable people out there, perhaps? No… it was something deeper than that. Something about how she felt when he was holding *her*? Whatever it was, it was touching something very deep in his own chest and…and it almost hurt. It also made it very hard to break that eye contact. He might still be sinking into that astonishing blueness if Peggy hadn't cleared her throat from the other side of the room.

'So…' There was amusement in her voice. 'That's how it is now for you two…'

It was actually more than amusement that Ari could hear coating her words. More than satisfaction that something she'd been angling for had finally happened. It was…it was joy, wasn't it? A deep, genuine happiness, as if she'd been gifted something that she'd set her heart on a long time ago and that was about the best thing Ari could have wished for Peggy to have in her life right now. And to be able to keep for as long as possible.

He couldn't tell her that the new closeness between himself and Kelly was only a temporary thing and it would never be a part of his long-term future. Peggy didn't need to know that. It would be far better if she could spend whatever time she had left on earth believing that he had someone as amazing as Kelly Reynolds to share his life with. That he had the prospect of his own family and happiness in his future.

Kelly had been startled into pretending that she was really focused on looking at some of the other photos on the corkboard but there were spots of colour on her cheeks that revealed her understanding of everything Peggy had expressed in just a few words. And when her gaze slipped back to his, as he pinned the new photo in place, he could see that she understood what he had been thinking as well.

At that moment, it appeared that a silent

pact was being made. They weren't going to say or do anything that might undermine Peggy's happiness. As far as they were both concerned, they could keep up the appearance of being in a committed relationship for as long as necessary to spare Peggy any disappointment. It was a welcome agreement because it gave them permission to let them carry on with their new, intimate connection.

It also gave Ari the confidence that everything was going to be okay. That Kelly understood that there were no promises of forever. That it was Peggy who'd brought them together and, when she was gone, that bond would also most likely evaporate. There was relief for Ari as well. He didn't have to rake over his past or emotions. He wasn't falling in love with Kelly and she wasn't going to get dependent on him or ask for anything more than he was able to give.

What they had going on at the moment was just…well, it was just what it was. Something that they both needed at this point in their lives. Kelly because she was on the way to believing in herself and maybe for him this was just a part of what he'd always been drawn to do—to make the vulnerable feel protected. Safe. To give them the gift of having hope for the future.

And if it came with the bonus of mind-blowingly amazing sex?

It was Ari's turn to clear his throat. Peggy certainly didn't need to know anything about that but it was a worry that she had seen so much already by simply witnessing a look between them. Was she seeing rather too much or was it too easy to see because there was more there than Ari was aware of?

Whatever Peggy was thinking now, however, was hidden beneath a carefully casual demeanour as she packed Kelly's squares, some new balls of wool and a crochet hook into a bag.

'Did you drive here today, lovey?'

'No, I caught the bus. So much easier than fighting late-afternoon London traffic.'

Peggy smiled. 'There'll be queues at the bus stops now, though, with people heading home from work. Ari—why don't you take Kelly home on that bike of yours?'

Ari almost shook his head. The suggestion was about as subtle as when Peggy had suggested he invite Kelly home for dinner that time. It was kind of funny now that he'd been so determined not to pass on that invitation because he hadn't wanted to complicate his life any more. Fate had had other ideas, hadn't she?

'It might take a while, even when I can get through most traffic on a bike,' Ari warned. 'It might be past your dinner and bedtime when I get back.'

Peggy was still smiling. 'That's perfect. I want a chance to talk to Stacey about a few things and we can do that over dinner—woman to woman. Then we can have a look on the internet and make a plan about how she could get the qualifications she would need for a job working with children. I don't want her to lose that dream.'

Ari found himself nodding slowly. It would be a very positive thing for Stacey to see something more in her future than being a teenage mother and, given the way she was inclined to push him away at times, like she had only minutes ago, a one-to-one talk with Peggy might achieve more. Peggy certainly seemed pleased with his agreement. Was it his imagination or did he also see her give him the ghost of a wink?

'I won't expect you back anytime soon, love,' she said serenely. 'London traffic is just terrible these days, isn't it?'

* * *

This was about Peggy's seal of approval that Kelly's friendship with Ari had become something more significant. There was a twinkle in her eyes when she kissed Kelly goodbye that made her realise she was only just getting to know a woman who had an endless capacity for living life to the fullest and trying to make it better for others at the same time. How lucky had she been to meet Peggy? And how easy was it to love her this much?

They got through the late afternoon traffic with ease as Ari slipped past the queued cars, trucks and buses at congested intersections. Pressed against his body, Kelly could feel every ripple of his muscles as he tilted even slightly in one direction and then the other and how her own body picked up those ripples and intensified them. She could have just handed Ari her helmet to put in the pannier of his bike and then gone into her basement flat alone but she caught his gaze as she stood beside him to pull the helmet from her head.

Her body was still buzzing from the contact they'd had even through their clothing and there was no way she was going into her flat alone if there was another option. Not just because Peggy had practically asked for time to be alone with Stacey but because the pull between them had just ignited something too powerful to even think about fighting.

They were down the steps even before Ari had pulled his helmet off properly and it was being dropped on the floor as Kelly turned—so quickly that she was already pressed against the solid warmth of his body. The flames of desire that were being fanned kicked up to a white heat as Ari cupped Kelly's face in his hands and covered her lips with his own.

She heard the front door slam shut and realised that Ari must have shoved it with his foot and then Kelly forgot about anything other than the touch of Ari's lips and his tongue and that those clever hands were slipping down her neck to her shoulders and beneath her clothing to find that deliciously sensitive, soft skin at the top of her breasts. Nothing else was going to enter her consciousness for quite some time and that was just perfect. The sound Kelly made as

Ari scooped her into his arms to carry her to her bed was one of absolute pleasure. Ecstasy, even…

Ripples of that bliss were still trickling through Kelly's body much later, as she stayed within the circle of Ari's arms, her face against the side of his chest where she could hear his heartbeat and feel his breathing finally settling to a normal range.

'Thank goodness for that bad London traffic,' she murmured.

The rumble of sound from Ari was amused. And full of fondness. 'She's a character, isn't she?'

'She's wonderful. I love her to bits.' The beat of sadness was enough to bring tears to Kelly's eyes. 'I hope… I hope I get a lot more time to get to know her better.'

Ari's arm tightened around her before relaxing slowly. 'It's impossible to say. Like a lot of stuff in life, we need to make the most of it while we have it.'

'Mmm…' Kelly had to swallow hard. He wasn't just talking about losing Peggy, was he? Was he warning her that times like this were also something they needed to make the most of because they weren't going to last very long?

The silence hung there as if they were both thinking the same thing. It was Ari who broke it.

'You're amazing, Kel,' he said softly. 'Don't let anyone ever make you believe that isn't true. Ever. Okay? Don't ever think you're not special enough to deserve the best because you are. You're the most amazing person I've ever met.'

The knot forming in her belly wasn't renewed desire. It was more like tension. Fear, even, that Ari was about to tell her their time together was already over? But she could feel herself smiling at the same time.

'I think you've got the gift of making any woman feel special,' she murmured. It was so true. His touch could be gentle enough to feel reverent but then it could change into something that was so passionate you could believe it was what he was feeling and tasting that was inspiring it. And then, when you threw away any inhibitions to respond in ways you'd never imagined, he was with you all the way—encouraging that response. Revelling in it...

'You need to believe it, though. In here...'

Ari laid his hand on Kelly's breast. Over her heart. 'And you need to keep believing it, even when I'm not here to remind you.'

Oh…the trailing ends of that internal knot had just been given a sharp tug so that it tightened enough to cause real pain. She might be safe within the circle of Ari's arms right now but her time with him wasn't going to last as long as Kelly would want it to.

Which was, she realised with absolute certainty, for ever.

It wasn't just Peggy who was so easy to love. She'd recognised the trust that Ari had won from her as a form of love but somehow she'd delegated it to the kind of love you could have with a good friend. She'd seen it as a signpost pointing to a future where it might be possible to find the all-consuming "falling in love" kind of love that was so far above the level of even your best friends. The kind of love that made you so sure that you'd found your soul-mate. The person that you didn't want to live without. The lover that you wanted to wake up next to, every day, for the rest of your life.

It had been a signpost all right. But how could she not have seen that it was pointing straight towards Ari Lawson?

That *he* was that person?

That knot wasn't about to unravel but Kelly could feel the tightness loosen a little as Ari's hand shaped her breast and then he bent his head to let his lips take the place of his fingers and the tip of his tongue to taste her nipple. She caught her breath in a gasp—arching her back, even, at the searing intensity of that pleasure.

'That traffic…' Ari's voice was so low it was no more than a whispered growl. 'It's particularly bad today…'

CHAPTER NINE

THE TRAFFIC WAS so much lighter by the time Ari finally headed home it was a pleasure to get up enough speed to lean into the corners and feel the pressure of wind against his body. After the last couple of hours in Kelly's bed, he was still a little drunk on the delights of physical pleasure that had raised the bar of what he'd believed possible. Even a gust of wind could rekindle the buzz. He knew it wasn't going to last that long—his sexual relationships never did—but, right now, Ari couldn't imagine not having Kelly in his life. He could never have had enough of her—in bed or out of it.

Daylight was beginning to fade so it was easy to spot the flashing lights of a police car coming up behind him as he got closer to home. A second police car wasn't far behind, its lights flashing and the siren also wailing.

When an ambulance rushed past him only a minute later, Ari knew that something major must be happening in his neighbourhood. A serious car crash perhaps? A stabbing or shooting?

It wasn't just in his neighbourhood either. The emergency vehicles were congregating in his own street. Right in front of his own house…? It was only then that any remnants of the delights of being with Kelly evaporated completely and fear kicked in to take their place. Ari was off his bike in a flash, running down the street as he yanked his helmet off.

'Sorry, sir, but you can't go in.' A policeman was blocking the path to the front door of the house. 'There's been an incident.'

'I live here.' Ari's words were clipped. 'My mother's in there. You can't stop me.'

He pushed past the officer, only to find another guarding the front door. Behind him, in the hallway, he could see an ambulance stretcher. Waiting for Peggy? Or was Stacey having her baby and something had gone wrong? But why were the police here as well as an ambulance?

'What the hell is going on here?'

The question was fired at the second officer but Ari didn't wait for an answer because he was too desperate to see for himself. Maybe this officer had heard him tell the one at the gate that he lived here. Or perhaps it was just the expression on his face that made the policeman step aside to let him in. Ari burst into the kitchen to find Stacey sitting at the table, flanked by two police officers. She was white-faced and sitting as still as a stone and it didn't look as if she was about to willingly communicate with anyone.

What was far more alarming, however, was the crumpled figure on the floor in front of the couch where he'd left Peggy resting comfortably some time ago. Two paramedics were crouched beside a body so still that, for a horrible moment, Ari thought that his mum was dead. He dropped to his knees close to her head but couldn't speak for a moment. He had to focus on taking a breath.

'Ari…' Peggy's voice was weaker than he'd ever heard it to be, even straight after her major surgery. 'Is that you? Oh…thank goodness you're here…'

Peggy's skin was even paler than Stacey's, except for where it was stained by a livid bruise appearing all around an eye that was already almost closed by swelling. Her lip was badly cut as well.

'Blood pressure's still too low,' one of the paramedics said. 'Let's get an IV in and get moving. How's that ECG looking?'

'Sinus rhythm,' his colleague responded. 'But tachycardic.' He looked up at Ari. 'And you are…?'

'He's my boy,' Peggy whispered. Her breath caught in a gasp that could have been either pain or fear. 'I need him…'

Ari had to swallow a huge lump in his throat. 'What's going on?' He had his hand on Peggy's forehead, smoothing back her hair. 'Did she fall? She's just come out of hospital after major abdominal surgery.'

'She didn't fall.' The senior paramedic shook his head. 'Some lowlife assaulted her. He was after drugs that he knew she had in the house, presumably because of the surgery.' His glance slid sideways and his tone hardened. 'Seems like he was a "friend" of the young lady living here.'

Peggy's unswollen eye was fluttering shut. 'Not her fault…' she whispered. 'Ari…you'll take care of Stacey, won't you?'

'Yeah…' But Ari had to push down a rising anger as he remembered the feverish text conversation he'd seen Stacey having before he'd left to take Kelly home. Had she been setting up the visit that had turned vicious? Had she deliberately put Peggy in danger by allowing a drug addict into the house? The abusive boyfriend that Kelly had told him about maybe? 'I'm going to take care of you first, though.'

But he needed to move back to give the paramedics room to work and he could feel the glare coming from the direction of the kitchen table. Anger bubbled and began to colour his words.

'What the hell were you thinking, Stace? Did you even think what the repercussions might be if you let your drug-addict mates know what was in the house? The medications that Peggy needs?'

Stacey said nothing. Her arms were wrapped tightly around her body above the bump of her pregnancy. She looked terrified beneath her resentment, Ari realised. And so, so young… He had to swallow hard.

'Are you okay?' he asked. 'Did he hit you as well?'

His anger might not have penetrated Stacey's stony silence but the concern in his voice did now. Not that Stacey seemed to appreciate his concern.

'As if you care,' she spat. 'You said you'd come back to look after Peggy. You promised you'd help look after *me*, too, but you're not that interested any more, are you?' Her lips curled as she glared at Ari. 'This wouldn't have happened if you'd been here but you weren't, were you? You were too busy, off shagging your girlfriend.'

Oh… *God*…the truth in those words was inescapable. This *was* his fault as much as Stacey's. What had he been thinking to let Kelly take over so much of the free time he had away from work when he should have been spending it caring for the closest thing to family he would ever have? The guilt that slammed into Ari on top of his fear for Peggy was too much. Ari could feel the pressure suddenly build to a point where he had to lash out.

'Who told that scumbag there were drugs in the house, Stace? What were you doing— trying to make a bit of pocket money?' He lowered his voice so that Peggy couldn't possibly hear if she was still conscious. 'If Peggy dies because of this, I'll never forgive you…'

He could see Stacey shrinking. Holding herself even more tightly, her lips now pressed together so hard they had all but vanished.

'What do you know about the person who might have carried out this attack?' the police officer asked Ari.

He shook his head. 'I only know that she's got a so-called boyfriend who's been abusive to her in public. And she had a friend over here for dinner not long ago.'

The night he'd first made love to Kelly, in fact. If he'd gone home that night, would he have met that "friend"? Could he have made it clear he wasn't welcome?

'Was it the same person, Stacey?' the policeman asked.

Stacey shrugged one shoulder but then nodded.

'Did you give him drugs then, too?'

Stacey ignored him.

'I can give you the name of a friend who saw him with her a while back,' Ari told the police officer. 'She'll be able to give you a description.'

'That could be helpful, although we've got a fair idea of who it is. Stacey's been doing her best to give us the information we need and we're confident he's someone who's already on our radar. You might want to know that he broke into the house because he was refused entry. And it was Stacey who called us to report the incident.'

And he'd just laid the blame on Stacey. Because he didn't want to face up to his own share? He'd known all along that he didn't have the room for any more complications in his life but he'd let Kelly in and devoted more and more of the precious time to being with her. But there was no point in trying to apportion blame right now. There was something far more important to worry about. Ari's head swerved back to where the paramedics were still working to stabilise Peggy for transport to hospital. A police officer was being used to hold up a bag of IV fluid. He could see a slightly erratic green line on the screen that was recording Peggy's heart rate and rhythm and equipment was being hastily collected and packed as if it was urgent to get her to hospital as quickly as possible.

Stacey's chair tipped backwards and toppled to the floor as she pushed herself to her feet.

'Don't go anywhere,' the police officer told her. 'We've still got a few more questions.'

'I need to go to the toilet.' Stacey's voice was wooden. 'If that's all right with you?'

'Of course.'

She didn't look in Ari's direction as she left the kitchen but he barely noticed. The stretcher had been brought into the room and the paramedics were being as gentle as they could as they lifted Peggy from the floor and arranged blankets and pillows around the wires of the ECG monitor and the tubing for the IV fluid. Ari could see the trace that told him Peggy was still alive but, looking at that pale, still face and the limp hand on top of the blankets, Ari felt the hollow space in his gut growing into an abyss. He was going to lose the person who'd been the most important to him for so much of his life—maybe a lot sooner than he'd expected.

'I'm coming with you,' he told the paramedics. 'I don't want her to be alone for a minute.'

'No worries. But let's get going, yeah?'

It took a minute to manoeuvre the stretcher through the kitchen door and into the hall, where they were blocked by two police officers.

'She's gone,' one of them was saying.

'What? How did that happen?'

'I couldn't go into the bathroom with her, could I? How was I to know that she was going to climb out the window…?'

They stepped aside to let the stretcher pass. Ari slowed as he followed it. 'Stacey's gone?'

'Done a runner.' The officer nodded. 'But don't worry, she can't have gone far, especially in her condition. We'll find her. Dunno why she's taken off when it's not her that's in trouble.'

Ari simply mirrored the nod. Stacey had stormed off because of what he'd said but right now he couldn't worry about the fact that he'd upset her so much—he had to focus on Peggy because, as awful as the thought was, it was quite possible these were the last minutes he would ever have with her. He lengthened his stride to catch up with the stretcher.

'I'm going to the hospital with my mother,' he threw back over his shoulder. 'You can find me there if you need to.'

He held her hand all the way to Kensington Hospital's emergency department. He was still holding it, more than an hour later, when she'd been admitted to a ward.

She was conscious again and he'd been

told that her being admitted was more of a precaution than anything else but he'd never seen Peggy looking like this. So old and shaky. As if life was finally just too hard. It was so typical of his mum that it wasn't herself that she was worried about, however.

'Please, Ari…go and find her. She's probably frightened. It wasn't her fault, you know. Not really…'

'I'd rather stay here. With you.'

Peggy shook her head but the movement made her wince. Her black eye was still swelling and changing colour and it looked horrific. She could see him staring.

'This looks far worse than it is. And after what they've given me, nothing hurts if I don't move. I'm going to sleep, Ari. There's no point in sitting by my bed, love. I'd much rather you went to find Stacey.' A tear escaped the eye that had been closed by the swelling and the whispered words might not have been intended to be heard. 'I don't want to die before I know she's all right… And that poor wee baby—what if it gets born on the streets…?'

So Ari went home. Because he'd decided he could collect Stacey and bring her back. The least she could do was to come into the hospital, no matter how much she disliked the place, to give Peggy the reassurance that would allow her to rest and try to heal from injuries that had to have set her back considerably in her recovery from the surgery.

But Stacey hadn't been found and taken home. The police officer that had been left to secure the house just shook his head at Ari's questions.

'There's too many places street kids can hide out in and that boyfriend of hers probably knows them all. If she doesn't want to be found, it's going to be very difficult.'

Ari paced the kitchen minutes later, the reminders of what had happened all too obvious, from some discarded packaging of IV supplies to blood spots on the polished floorboards and the odd angle of the chair Stacey had knocked over that had been picked up but not straightened.

"Difficult" didn't mean you couldn't try, but he didn't know where to start and…and Ari had never felt so alone in his life. Or maybe that wasn't quite true. He'd felt rather like this as an abandoned six-year-old, hadn't he? When what he'd needed most of all had been someone to love him. Someone who would put their arms around him and tell him everything was going to be okay. There was only one person he could think of who might be able to make him feel less alone.

He pulled his phone from his pocket without giving himself time to think it through and the warmth that flooded his body the instant he heard Kelly's voice told him that he'd been right. She *was* the person he needed most right now. He had to fight back tears as he told her what had happened and his need to try and do something to fix everything but the frustration of not knowing where to start.

'I know a few places street kids hang out in,' she told him. 'I've gone there on ambulance jobs. There's an under-bridge homeless community not far from Kensington Hospital that I've been to. And an old house not far from you. I went there for a drug overdose once.'

'What street is it in?'

'I can't remember the name. I'd know it if I saw it, though, and roughly where the street is. Come and get me, Ari. I'll help you look…'

It felt good to be on the back of this bike because it gave her an excuse to wrap her arms around Ari and hold him tightly. It couldn't have felt more different than the last time she'd been on the back of his bike only hours ago, however, when she'd been aware of every tiny movement of his muscles. Even through the protective layer of that leather jacket over his clothing now she could feel how tense he was—a solid mass of focused human who was probably barely aware of the touch of her arms.

Kelly would have been beyond appalled to learn about a cowardly attack involving physical violence on any frail, old woman but this was Peggy and that made it utterly unthinkable. While she was inclined to agree with Ari's first reaction and blame Stacey for what had happened, she could understand how torn he was and how important it was for Peggy to know that the teenager was all right. Stacey had listened to Kelly once when she'd told her how lucky she was to have Peggy and Ari in her life and it had apparently made a difference so maybe she could help again. She desperately wanted to help. For Peggy, of course, and for Stacey herself but mostly for Ari. The haunted look on his face when he'd arrived to collect her on his bike had been heart-breaking.

As far as they could tell, Stacey wasn't

amongst the group of homeless young people who had claimed the area under the bridge that Kelly knew about.

'Have you seen her?' Ari asked someone who had dreadlocks reminiscent of the hairstyle he'd had when he was seventeen. 'She's got really bright red hair, short on one side. And she's pregnant.'

'Nah, man…she's not here. No one's seen her.'

People were turning their backs on them.

'If you do see her, tell her Ari's looking for her. Tell her to come home.'

They got an even more hostile reception at the abandoned house that was inhabited by squatters—many of whom were no older than Stacey.

'You're not in trouble,' Kelly told whoever had been swearing at her on the other side of the closed door. 'We need to find someone, that's all. Stacey. Red hair. She's pregnant and the baby could come anytime.'

'We've already had the cops here and I reckon that's your fault.' The door opened a crack. 'Get lost or you'll be sorry…'

For some time after that, they rode around the streets, slowing to check shadowy doorways or lanes and stopping when they saw a figure walking alone or hunched on a park bench. It grew later. And colder. Kelly could feel the tension mounting as the realisation sank in that they were looking for a needle in a haystack, trying to find a single teenaged girl in a city of millions of people. There were lines on Ari's face she'd never seen before and he was so focused on his search he didn't even meet her eyes or seem to hear things she said.

It was a tacit acknowledgment that their efforts were futile when Ari finally took Kelly back to her flat. He took his helmet off to talk to her when she'd climbed off the back but he stayed sitting astride the bike as if he wanted to be ready to take off at a moment's notice.

Kelly wanted so badly to try and reassure him. Even if the only thing she could do was to hold him and keep him company.

'Come in. I'll make some coffee.'

'Nah… I'm going to keep looking for a while. Then I'll go back and see how Mum is.'

'I'll come with you.'

'I've already arranged time off work.' Ari still wasn't meeting her gaze. 'You've got an early shift tomorrow and there's no point staying up all night anyway. Like the police said, if she doesn't want to be found, it's going to be difficult.'

'She'll come back,' Kelly told him. 'I'm sure of it.'

'Why would she? She's as upset as any of us and she blames me. She said it wouldn't have happened if I'd been at home and she's right. I would have flattened that bastard before he got anywhere near Mum.'

'I know.' The words were hard to get out. She did know just how protective Ari would have been. She also knew that the reason Ari hadn't been at home was because he'd been with *her*. In her bed. Making love to her that second time… He was blaming himself now. Was he blaming her as well?

'I knew how she felt and I ignored it,' Ari said softly. Finally, he did meet her gaze and the pain she could see in his eyes was unbearable. 'This is more my fault than hers. 'Do you remember—that first time you came to dinner?'

Kelly nodded. Of course she remembered. 'It was when Peggy gave me my first knitting lesson.'

And when Stacey had totally dismissed the idea of her being Ari's girlfriend but she'd known that Peggy was hoping something was going to happen between them—almost as much as Kelly was?

'I almost didn't invite you,' Ari admitted. 'I knew I shouldn't get any closer to you because…well, because I can't do long term and you deserve better than a relationship that isn't going anywhere but, more than that, I knew I owed it to Mum and Stacey not to get involved with someone who was going to distract me from what I'd come back to London for in the first place—to look after Mum. I didn't know Stacey was in trouble but, as soon as I did, I had to look out for her as well.'

'Of course you did. They're your family.' Kelly was still holding her helmet in her arms. Hugging it when she would far rather be hugging Ari.

'I knew how attracted I was,' he continued. 'But I actually believed that we could be friends. I knew that was how it had to be because Stacey reminded me that night. She was really sulky and let me know that it was because she thought you were my girlfriend. And I reassured her. I said, "As if I've got time for a girlfriend when I've got you and Mum to look after at the moment."'

Kelly was biting her bottom lip now. So hard that it hurt. She'd played her own part in all of this. She'd wanted more than friendship. She'd wanted Ari to kiss her that first time so badly that when it hadn't happened, the disappointment had been crushing. She'd wanted it all.

She still did, but she could feel it disappearing. Being gently but irrevocably being taken away from her.

'We can't be "just friends", can we?' I can't be anywhere near you, Kel, without wanting more. Without it messing with my head so much it's too hard to think of anything else. Well…work's okay…' He met her gaze for a heartbeat and there was even a hint of a smile on his face. 'Better than okay, really, because when I'm working with you, it feels like I can do more than I ever could on my own.'

Kelly was nodding. 'I know. I feel the same way.'

Ari's breath came out in an audible sigh. 'Yeah…we make an amazing team but, out of work, it's a different story. For me anyway. If we'd been able to keep our hands off each other, I would have got home in time to make sure this never happened. It *shouldn't* have happened.' The anger in his tone was chilling. 'None of it.'

Kelly's throat was so tight it was hard to take a breath. Or to release any more words but they came out anyway. Because she had to know.

'Including me?' Her voice cracked. 'Us?'

He held her gaze properly this time and there was no way on earth Kelly could have broken it.

'I've never asked for relationships in my life,' Ari said quietly. 'Never expected them. Not after my mother just dumped me and walked out. I never wanted them, I guess, because I knew how they ended. But Peggy just happened and so did Stacey and it feels like I had no choice but to love them—as if the love had always been there for me to find, or something. I have to be there for them and, to do that, I can't be with you. I'm sorry... You're the last person I'd ever want to hurt.'

Or maybe not the last person because there were others who were more important? But Kelly could see the turmoil in those dark eyes—the agony of the loss of his mum that he might be facing, anger for a foster sister he'd held when she was just a newborn baby, that was confused by a compassion he couldn't banish and…and just pain. Even if he loved her as much as she knew she loved him, he had to push her away, didn't he? Because there were others that he felt responsible for. People he cared about who had been in his life a lot longer than she had. She had to respect that.

And, because Kelly loved him that much, she could do the one thing that help him at the moment. She could let him go and make at least this part of the mess easier to fix.

'It's okay, Ari,' she said softly. 'It's going to be okay.'

'How?'

'You'll find Stacey. You can do what you came back for and look after your mum and you don't need to let anything else interfere with that. Maybe, one day, we can be just friends…' Kelly handed Ari her helmet. She needed to get away. To duck down the steps to her flat and out of sight before she started crying. 'If that's something we both want.'

This was unbearable. There were echoes from the past that were trying to gain head space. Darryn's voice…

'You're a useless lump… Waste of time… Dunno what I ever saw in you in the first place…'

She had already turned away when Ari said something so she couldn't be quite sure what she'd heard but if it was agreement about wanting some kind of relationship in the future, it sounded too tentative to be of any comfort.

'Maybe…one day…'

CHAPTER TEN

Being nothing more than friends didn't mean you weren't allowed to care.

Kelly's priority the next day, at the first opportunity she had with a break in her shift, was to visit Peggy in a ward of Kensington Hospital where she'd been admitted for observation and further assessment of her traumatic injuries. It was no surprise to find Ari sitting by her bed, holding his mum's hand, even though she appeared to be asleep, but it was almost overwhelming to find how hard this was going to be—to let Ari go like this. To step back and turn away from a love that she could feel burning in every cell of her body.

He looked as if he'd slept even less than she had last night. Paler than normal skin made his eyes look almost black and the knot of hair high on the back of his head was messy enough to have fronds escaping on all sides. Kelly could see—or perhaps feel—the tension in his body, even though he smiled at her as she came into the private room Peggy had been given. What she wanted, more than anything, was to walk straight into his arms and just hold him as tightly as she could for a few seconds, to let him know how much her heart was aching for him and that she could be by his side for every moment of this ordeal if it would help.

It wouldn't help, though, would it? Their being together was the reason Ari was blaming himself for the terrible thing that had happened to Peggy. He had let down the most important person in his life in the worst way possible and she knew Ari well enough to understand that he had to take control somehow now and put things right. That he had to care for the people he loved. And she loved him enough to let that happen, even if it meant that she might lose him for ever.

He didn't meet her gaze for more than a heartbeat as he offered her that smile of welcome. His attention shifted almost instantly and it was obvious it was slipping straight back to where it had been, probably for many hours—to Peggy's face.

'How is she?' Kelly kept her voice low. Rest was going to be vital for Peggy's physical healing. Having Ari by her side would be equally vital for her emotional healing but how hard was it going to be to get over such an appalling attack? In her own home and when she had been with someone she deserved to be able to trust?

'There's no sign of a significant head injury and she doesn't seem to have suffered any internal injuries from the fall but they're going to keep a careful eye on her for a day or two.' Ari rubbed his forehead with his free hand and his voice was raw. 'She was only just starting to heal from the surgery.'

'I know…' Kelly swallowed the lump in her throat.

'They caught him. The police came in this morning.' Ari sounded as if it didn't really matter now. 'He was out on the streets, trying to sell the tramadol he'd nicked. He's been arrested. He probably won't be out of prison and able to hurt anyone else for a very long time.'

Maybe it didn't actually matter so much to Ari now because the damage had already been done to someone who was precious to him. Damage he should have been able to prevent. If anybody could take any blame for this atrocity, it had to be Stacey, but Ari felt responsible for her as well, didn't he? He probably had, to some degree, ever since he'd held her when she'd been a tiny, vulnerable baby having a rough start in life. And Kelly couldn't begrudge the place the troubled teenager had in his life. It was one of the things she loved about him, after all— that extraordinary ability to love and protect. The quality of being someone you could trust with your life.

And your heart…if he let you get that close.

'Have they found Stacey, too?'

Ari shook his head. 'No sign of her.'

As if she'd heard the whispered name, Peggy's eyelids fluttered.

'Stacey?'

'No sign yet, Ma.' Ari leaned closer to rest the backs of his fingers gently on Peggy's cheek. 'Try not to worry, yeah? They'll find her. I'll go back out to look again later, too, when I know you're going to get some proper sleep. I'll pop home first. Who knows? Maybe she's there and tucked up in her own bed again.'

'Oh…' Peggy still hadn't opened her eyes. 'Go now, Ari. Please…go and check…'

'Soon. I'm not going anywhere just yet. I've got all the time I need away from work. I'm not leaving you.'

'I'm on the road all day,' Kelly added. 'I'll be looking out for Stacey, too. I've already put the word out for any other ambulance officers to help. It's a good thing that she's so easy to recognise with that hair of hers.'

'Oh…' Peggy opened her eyes properly as her head turned towards Kelly. 'You're here too, lovey. I'm so pleased about that…'

'I had to come and see how you were.' Kelly stepped closer to the bed. 'I'm so, so sorry this has happened to you, Peggy.' The threat of tears muffled her words and Kelly could feel a stab of the horrible guilt that she knew Ari was struggling with right now— that she had been in his arms, in blissful ignorance, happier than she'd ever been in her life, while this unthinkable attack had happened to the sweetest old woman she had ever met.

'It's not the worst thing in the world.' Peggy's voice had a wobble in it. 'I'm more worried about our Stacey and that baby of hers. And you,' she added, turning back to Ari.

'You've got to stop blaming yourself, love. This isn't your fault.' Her head sank back into the pillow and her eyes were closing. 'Thank goodness you've got Kelly. She'll look after you...'

Except that Ari didn't want to be looked after. He was the one who looked after others and nothing was going to be allowed to interfere with that any more.

Kelly could almost feel the wall between them and she suddenly realised why his relationships had never lasted. He was the person who could be needed, and relied on, and he would always be there for the people who'd captured his heart, like Peggy and Stacey. But he would never willingly become the needy one, relying on someone else, where you could have your own trust—and your heart—shattered.

Her heart ached for the small boy he'd once been, when that ability to trust had been ripped away when his mother had abandoned him. And it ached even more for the beautiful man he was now, but she couldn't push any closer in emotional terms at the moment because she knew it would only make him run harder and faster and then she might lose sight of him for ever.

Even if…and possibly entirely due to the fact that he felt the connection between them as much as Kelly did. Perhaps he actually loved her already but couldn't admit it. Because it made him too vulnerable? It wasn't possible to force someone to trust you. Maybe Peggy was the only person on earth that Ari would ever trust to that degree. He was facing the loss of something incredibly precious but Kelly couldn't offer him any comfort because being too close would only make it harder for him.

She bent to place a very gentle kiss on Peggy's cheek. 'I'll be back to see you later,' she said. 'Rest and get better, okay?'

Ari looked up as she straightened and, for a brief moment that seemed to stretch for ever, the silent communication encompassed everything that had been running through Kelly's mind. The guilt and the fear of loss, the trauma of the past that made it impossible to trust, the need to care for others and… there seemed to be a heartfelt apology there as well.

It felt like a goodbye and it left a haunting note that stayed with Kelly as her afternoon wore on with call after call to people needing help from the ambulance service.

To make it even harder it seemed that fate was making sure that every job had something about it that made her think of the new, significant people in her life. A cyclist had been clipped by a car not far from the charity shop where she'd bought those balls of wool—and seen Stacey being abused by her boyfriend. The elderly lady who was struggling for breath because her heart failure had taken a turn for the worse had silver hair just like Peggy's and there was something about the way that young father was holding his baby in his arms on her last call for the day that reminded her so much of that photo of Ari holding Stacey as a baby.

Except it wasn't quite her last call for the day. The febrile seizure that had terrified the baby's father had not been repeated but Kelly had called for back-up to take them to hospital for further assessment, monitoring and much-needed reassurance. Her radio crackled as she headed back to her station.

'Rover One, please respond to call for back-up from police. You're the closest unit to the bridge on Campbell Road, south of Kensington Hospital. Person threatening to jump.'

Kelly hit the switch to start her beacons

flashing. She blipped her siren as well, to warn traffic as she made a U-turn and then sped towards the bridge. Following the theme of her afternoon, this job was also going to remind her of Ari because the area beneath that bridge was one of the places they had gone to last night to search for Stacey. A bridge that had high steel curves on either side. If someone had climbed up to the top of the curve, they could fall onto the roadway instead of the river, which would be un-survivable. Kelly could feel the tension increasing rapidly as she neared the bridge to see the flashing lights of police cars blocking traffic from using the bridge.

Worse, she recognised the silhouette of one of the police officers standing by his car, his feet planted wide and his arms folded as he formed part of the barricade. Darryn. The last person she wanted to see anywhere but particularly today when she was already feeling the loss so poignantly of what might have been with Ari. Clearly Darryn didn't feel the same antipathy.

'Hey, Cowbell. Can't stay away from me, huh?'

Kelly ignored him, walking past to find whoever was in charge of this scene. She was looking up and her heart sank as she saw that someone had, indeed, climbed up the latticework of steel. They weren't near the top but they were still high enough for a fall to be potentially fatal, whether it was into the river or onto the roadway.

'Don't go too close, darling.' Darryn's voice was teasing enough to be uncomfortably familiar but the undertone was anything but affectionate. 'She might take one look at you and decide to jump. Two for the price of one, there, too.'

'What?' Kelly's head swerved. 'What's that supposed to mean?'

Darryn tapped the side of his head. 'Thought you were smarter than that, Cowbell. The driver that called this in saw her start climbing. She's got a bun in the oven.'

Kelly was shading her eyes with her hand, trying to see into the fading daylight against the over-bright lights of emergency vehicles around her. Maybe there wasn't enough light to see hair colour or the bump of a pregnant belly but Kelly's heart took another dive as she reached for her phone. She just knew that this was Stacey.

She hit a speed dial button on her phone, spoke only for seconds and then headed behind the police vehicles towards where the curved side of the bridge started its rise on the other side of some railings. There were two sides to the curve connected by steel pipes that looked enough like a ladder to suggest it would be easy to climb.

'Don't go any closer.' A police officer wearing a "Scene Commander" high-vis vest came swiftly in Kelly's direction. 'We've tried talking to her and she said she'll jump if anyone tries to climb up. We've got a police negotiator on the way. She's just a kid.'

'I'm pretty sure I know her,' Kelly told him. 'And I've got a family member on his way.'

More than on his way, in fact. Ari must have run like the wind from the hospital to have got to this bridge so fast. He was out of breath but it didn't stop him cupping his hands to try and make his voice carry further.

'Stace? Don't move… I'm coming up to get you.'

'*No…*' The sound was faint but unmistakable. 'Stay away…'

Ari shook his head. 'No way…' He could have been talking to himself as he eyed the railing and the structure of the curves. 'This is my fault. I can fix this…'

'You're not going up there,' the police commander told him. 'I'm not going to risk escalating this situation. We just need to wait until—' He stopped talking abruptly as another call came from above.

'What?' He shouted. 'Say that again?'

'Kelly…' Again, the words were faint but audible. 'I want to talk to Kelly.'

Kelly could feel everybody staring at her, including Darryn, but she was only looking back at one person. Ari. Holding his gaze. She knew exactly how desperate he was to get closer to Stacey to make sure she could be kept safe. She knew how hard it would be—impossible, perhaps—for him to trust someone else with something this important. She took a step closer and kept holding that dark gaze. Trying with all her might to convince him that she would never do anything to hurt him. Ever…

'Trust me, Ari,' she said softly. 'Please…'

'Yeah, right…' The taunting tone could only have come from one person. 'Wouldn't do that if I was you, mate…'

Kelly head snapped around to face Darryn. 'Shut up,' she told him. 'You're not only being completely unprofessional, you're showing everyone what an abusive bully you are. And you know what?' She didn't wait for any response. 'You don't intimidate me in the slightest.'

And he didn't, she realised. What had Ari said about working with her? That it felt as if he could do more than he ever could on his own? She felt the same way. She had more courage and confidence when she had Ari just standing close to her, let alone working with her. Even if the brief time they'd had together was all she'd ever have, Kelly would be grateful for the rest of her life for what he'd given her. It was this man who'd encouraged her to believe in herself—to believe in love—again.

Darryn—the abusive bully she'd been unfortunate to have had a relationship with—was never going to intimidate her again. Thanks to Ari, she was no longer afraid of this man on any level. She didn't even bother looking at him as she pushed past.

'Now…get out of my way.'

He'd seen her stand up to an aggressive man the first time they'd met and he'd been blown away by Kelly's courage. He'd also seen her shrink in the face of abuse from this man but here she was, standing up to him with just as much authority as she had dealt with Vicky's husband that day. Darryn was backing away, like the coward he probably was, and even amongst his fear for Stacey and the determination to be the one to protect her somehow and then get her to safety, he felt a burst of pride for Kelly and the satisfaction of realising that she was in the space he had wished for her to be in all along. A space where she could believe in herself and realise that she deserved so much better than anything a creep like Darryn could have offered her.

No wonder it was Kelly that Stacey wanted to talk to rather than him and, as hard as it was, Ari knew that he had to do what Kelly had asked him to do. He had to trust her. And it seemed like he wasn't the only one who was prepared to do that. The police officer in charge had a slightly stunned look on his face as he stood back to allow Kelly climb the railing and gain access to the edge of the bridge structure.

Her face was set in tight lines that Ari had seen before. In that car with Zoe when it had shifted on the rocks in that flood and, for a moment, they had faced the reality of how much danger they were in. When he'd held Kelly's gaze and tried to reassure her that he was going to do anything he could to protect her.

But he couldn't protect her now. Even though it was tearing him apart, there was nothing Ari could do but to stand here and watch.

And trust…

This was scarier than anything Kelly had ever had to do in her work. Scarier than being in a car in a flooded stream even, but she'd been able to find the courage to cope with that and she could find that same kind of courage now because…because Ari was nearby and that changed everything. Like he felt himself, they were better together than alone and that meant that Kelly could be a version of herself that was only possible because she believed it was. Because Ari believed she was amazing?

She had begged Ari to trust her and now she had to trust herself. She'd got through to Stacey once before by being honest and not holding back. Was that why Stacey wanted to talk to her now? Because she knew that she could trust Kelly to tell her the truth, even if it was difficult to hear?

'Don't come any closer. I could still jump...'

Oh, *God*... The fear in Stacey's voice was heart-breaking. Kelly had to fight back the threat of tears and it took a supreme effort to keep her voice calm.

'No, you won't,' she said quietly. 'You wouldn't do that. Not when it's going to hurt the people who care about you so much.'

'They don't care any more. Why would they? It's my fault that Peggy got hurt. Ari said so.'

'He was upset. People say things they don't necessarily mean when they upset. But they don't stop caring because something bad happens.' Kelly climbed another rung. 'I went to see Peggy today and you know what the only thing is that she's worrying about?'

Stacey was silent for a long moment but Kelly waited until she felt compelled to ask. To buy into the conversation.

'What?'

'You. You...and your baby. Ari's worried, too. He's down there on that bridge and he's holding his breath, waiting to see that you're okay. He wants to take you to see Peggy.

You're a family, you guys. You need to be together right now.' She climbed another rung and then two. 'I'm not just saying this stuff, Stacey. You know I'm telling you what's true.' She was almost close enough to touch Stacey, who was clinging to the framework of the steel curve, her eyes screwed shut and her face tear-streaked and pale.

'I can't...' Fresh tears were rolling down Stacey's cheeks. 'I can't go down.'

'You can.' Kelly swallowed her fear. 'I'm here. I'll help you.'

'No... I can't. My back hurts too much and...and I've wet my pants.'

'Oh...' Kelly closed the distance between them as much as she could. The gap between the two sides that made the curve was wide enough for her climb right up beside Stacey. To put her arm around the frightened teenager. 'You know what this probably means, don't you?'

Stacey's body was still rigid but she was leaning against Kelly as if she desperately needed the human contact. 'What?'

'Your baby might have decided it's time to arrive.' Kelly reached for her radio with her free hand, careful not to rock the weight Stacey was trusting her to support. 'There's a fire truck down there on the bridge with a long ladder and I think it's just become even more important that we get you safely back on the ground as fast as possible. Are you ready?'

'No…they're going to be mad at me…'

'Who? Ari? Peggy? Are you kidding? They love you. You can trust that, you know. Always…'

He had known, deep down, that he could trust Kelly.

Always.

It hadn't made it any easier to stand back and watch, however. It was, in fact, the first time that Ari could remember allowing himself to be so vulnerable. To have so much hanging on the outcome of trusting someone else.

He had been too far away to hear anything that was being said between Kelly and Stacey but he had felt the tension rising steadily as Kelly had climbed closer. And then she had her arm around Stacey and he heard her voice coming over the radio of the police officer in charge but, instead of relieving that tension, her words made Ari catch his breath in horror.

'We need the ladder and basket to get down.' Kelly sounded calm. 'And an ambulance called, please, if there isn't one on the way already. Stacey here is in labour. I don't think we're going to have time to get her up to ED at the Kensington.'

An ambulance arrived only minutes later, as the fire officers were getting both Kelly and Stacey safely into the basket on the top of the ladder. Ari watched it being lowered, the extendable ladder folding into itself until the basket landed gently on the ground. Ari was right beside it as the side was opened, ready to add his support to Kelly to get Stacey into the privacy of the ambulance. He could see how scared Stacey was and it was heart-breaking.

'It's okay,' he told her, holding out his arms. 'It's all going to be okay, I promise…'

Stacey took a step towards him but then stopped, crying out as she doubled over in pain. Ari caught her as she leaned so far forward it looked as if she might fall, scooping her up into his arms as if she weighed no more than a child. He carried her to the warmed cabin of the ambulance, with Kelly following close behind, and, seconds later, it was just the three of them in that secure space, with no room for the ambulance crew if it wasn't needed.

'Something's happening,' Stacey sobbed, as Ari put her down on the stretcher. She pulled her legs up as Kelly was peeling the purple dungarees clear. 'It feels weird. Like I have to…have to push…'

Ari had sterile gloves on already. 'Your baby's coming, Stace. I can see the head already. It's crowning.' He knew exactly what to do now to try and protect both Stacey and her baby. He didn't have to trust anybody else but he couldn't have wished for anyone other than Kelly to be by his side in these tense moments of trying to ensure that Stacey's baby arrived safely in the world.

'You're doing so well, Stacey,' Kelly told her. 'Good girl…'

'It hurts,' Stacey groaned. 'It's burning.'

'Don't push,' Ari told her. There was a risk of her tearing if she pushed right now. 'Take short, shallow breaths like this.' He showed her what he meant. 'Pretend you're blowing out a candle on a cake. And…' he took hold of Stacey's hand to direct it '…you can feel baby's head just here. See? That his hair that you're touching.'

'Oh… *Ohh*…' Stacey was touching her

baby's head but she was staring at Ari. 'It's real,' she choked out. 'A real baby...' Her words got swallowed by another cry of pain.

'You can push with this contraction,' Ari told her. 'Push as hard as you can...'

He checked to make sure the umbilical cord wasn't around the baby's neck as the head was born and then it took only minutes to coach Stacey through another contraction and catch the body of her baby as it appeared.

'It's a boy...' Ari had never been this close to tears at a birth before. He'd witnessed the miracle of it happening countless times and some of those births had been remarkable enough that he would never forget them—like delivering Zoe's baby in the car, for example, but this was something different again. This was the baby of someone he had cradled in his arms when she had been no more than a newborn herself. This was family and the love for this baby was already there.

Kelly had a soft towel ready to wrap the baby in and then they helped Stacey to take her son in her arms. And, as she cradled him, Ari met Kelly's gaze over the top of the baby and he recognised, in that moment, what had been there all along—he just hadn't let himself see it. He loved her. He had no more choice about loving Kelly Reynolds, in fact, than he'd had in his relationships with Peggy and Stacey.

It felt like his love for Kelly had always been there. How could he not have realised that Kelly had not only captured his heart virtually the moment he'd met her, but that she was the part of it that he'd been missing for ever. He'd felt that bond of trust and been amazed that he could achieve more in his work with her by his side than he could alone but this was more than that. Much, much more. This was about his whole life. His future.

And it seemed that perhaps Kelly understood the tsunami of emotion that was rushing through Ari in those intense seconds as Stacey gazed at her baby with total wonder and he was holding Kelly's gaze with a very similar kind of wonder as he began to see how much his universe had just changed. It certainly looked as if she was feeling exactly the same thing.

This moment—that Ari knew he would remember for ever—would have to be broken very soon. Stacey and her baby needed to be transferred to Kensington Hospital's emergency department to be checked and, as soon as they were cleared for discharge, there was an elderly woman in a ward upstairs who was going to be overjoyed to have her family gather in her room and to meet the newest member. The moment could be held for just a heartbeat longer, though, couldn't it? Enough time for one of those swift, silent conversations that he and Kelly could have from just sharing a long glance.

From letting their souls touch for a heartbeat.

I love you, his gaze told her. *I trust you. I trust us...*

And he could read her reply as easily as if she'd spoken aloud.

So do I. Always and forever...

EPILOGUE

Three years later...

'I wish Peggy was here.'

'Oh, but she is…' Kelly smiled up at Ari as she stood on tiptoe to kiss him softly. 'She's everywhere in this house. Don't you feel it?'

She saw his gaze shift to the battered old couch that was still at the end of the kitchen, still draped in those colourful blankets made from knitted squares. Currently it was bathed in sunlight streaming through the open French doors that led out to the garden.

'That's where you were looking after her,' Ari murmured. 'That day that you got called here.'

Kelly let her head tilt so that it was tucked into a favourite spot, just below his collar bone, as she stayed snug in the circle of his arms. 'You carried her to that couch,' she said softly. 'Do you know, I think that was the moment I started to fall in love with you? I wanted to be held like you were holding Peggy. To have someone who could make me feel that safe…that loved…'

Ari pressed a kiss to the top of her head. 'And do you?' he asked. 'Still?'

'More every day. Especially today…' Kelly's heart was filling again, so much that it brought tears to her eyes.

'I reckon I fell in love with you the moment I wanted to hold you like that.' She could feel the way Ari had to swallow hard. 'There you were, a kick-ass paramedic with a dodgy situation under total control and then, suddenly, I could see the person inside. The Kelly that *needed* someone to hold her like that. To tell her that she was the most amazing person in the world.'

Kelly really had to blink tears away now as she turned to look out towards the garden, where a small girl with brown eyes and blonde hair was trying to tie ribbons around the tail of a very patient, large dog. 'What do you think Maggie's going to say when we tell her she's going to get a little brother or sister?'

'I think she'll say she wants a brother. She adores Jack, doesn't she?'

'Who wouldn't? Stacey's doing such a wonderful job in bringing him up. Peggy would be so proud of her.'

'And of her graduating as a nursery teacher. She was so determined to see her succeed. I reckon that was what made her live so much longer than any of us expected. At least she got to celebrate Stacey getting all the GCSEs she needed from night school.'

Kelly was smiling again. 'She was just as determined that we would get together, too. If you hadn't passed on her dinner invitation it might never have happened.'

Ari's arms tightened around her. 'I can't imagine life if it hadn't happened. And Peggy was still well enough to dance at our wedding. Still there to meet Maggie the night she was born. To know that we had named her Margaret- after her.'

Kelly turned her face back to nestle against Ari and they held each other very tightly for a moment. It was such a poignant memory because that had been the night that Peggy had slipped away from them, not long after holding her precious new grandchild in her arms. She had died in her sleep, surrounded by her closest family. Surrounded by the kind of love that the walls of this house still embraced. So much love but there was still an infinite capacity for more.

Kelly didn't need to tell Ari how lucky she was feeling. Or how much she loved him and how excited she was to know that a new member of their family was on the way. All she had to do was look up and catch his gaze. It only took a moment for one of those lightning-fast silent conversations that could say everything that captured the past, present and future of those three little words.

I love you…

* * * * *